Too Cold for Snow

Jon Gower is a writer, performer and broadcaster whose work includes award-winning documentaries for radio, television and the internet. He has written fifteen books on subjects as diverse as a disappearing island in Chesapeake Bay – *An Island Called Smith* – which won the John Morgan award, *Real Llanelli* – a west Wales tour in psycho-geography – and the fiction of *Dala'r Llanw, Uncharted* and *Big Fish.* His most recent work of non-fiction is *The Story of Wales*, which accompanies a landmark TV series.

He writes in both Welsh and English, is a Creative Wales Award winner and is currently a Hay Festival International Fellow.

Jon lives in Cardiff, Wales with his wife Sarah and two daughters, Elena and Onwy.

Too Cold for Snow

Jon Gower

PARTHIAN

Parthian
The Old Surgery, Napier Street
Cardigan SA43 1ED
www.parthianbooks.com

First published in 2012

ISBN 978-1-908069-84-9

The publisher acknowledges the financial support
of the Welsh Books Council.

'Bunting' is the author's own translation of a story in Welsh that won the Short Story Prize at the National Eisteddfod in Cardiff in 2008.
'TV Land' first appeared in *Urban Welsh: New Welsh Fiction*, (Parthian, 2005) edited by Lewis Davies.
'The Pit' was included in the anthology *Sing Sorrow Sorrow*, (Seren, 2010) edited by Gwen Davies.
'Picture Perfect' first appeared under the title 'The Communist' in *Evan Walters: Moments of Vision* (Seren, 2011) edited by Barry Plummer.

Some of the stories in this volume were written courtesy of a bursary awarded by Academi, now called Literature Wales, which is gratefully acknowledged.

Edited by Eluned Gramich

Cover design by www.theundercard.com
Typesetting by Lucy Llewellyn

Printed and bound by www.lightningsource.com
British Library Cataloguing in Publication Data

A cataloguing record for this book is available from the British Library.

Contents

Bunting

My, she could whistle! After shedding the trappings of language, my eighty-year-old mother, Alaw, took to whistling, and not any old whistling either. She draped nightingale melodies around the utilitarian, steeped-in-piss furniture at the old people's home and it was so, well, *appropriate.* I am here, this is my place, observe me.

Luscinia megarhynchos. The nightingale. 'A medium sized songbird of shy and secretive habits with a discretely rufous tail.' A bird that sings so enthusiastically during moonlit hours it's been known to die in mid-warble.

It rated high as entertainment. If ever Tony Bennett cancelled a gig at Caesar's Palace you could have booked her in his place, although God only knows what the Las Vegas punters would have made of a fragile and rickety woman creaking her way onto the stage as an augmented orchestra struck up with something brassy. But if they'd been patient for just two minutes while she got her breath and adjusted her sticks – if they'd just sipped their cosmos and margaritas and their industrial-strength rusty nails, and just shut the fuck up, simply offered the old dear that much good grace – they'd have been transported. They'd have actually heard the music of the spheres, leaving the empty husks of their bodies behind to fly as iridescent dragonflies around the chandelier-lit room – swear to God they would – which surely had to be worth the price of admission? Worth five hundred bucks of anyone's money.

But her melodic brilliance – those glimmering notes, those pitch perfect descants, the rising scales that could be soundtracks for epiphanies – was confined to the tightly hemmed-in quarters of the home, where she was loved by residents and staff alike, but loved especially when she whistled. Whoo-ee-oo. Whoo-ee-oo.

There was never much silence in Noddfa, what with the barkers and shouters and screamers – all the cacophonous soundtrack of the Elderly Mentally Infirm. It was worse at night and worst on moonlit nights. The place sounded like a shearwater colony. In west Wales they call shearwaters cocklollies, to mimic their macabre calls. Someone once described the shearwater's call as it returns to land under cover of darkness as a rooster in full cry seconds after its throat has been cut. Imagine tens of thousands of seabirds all making that sound and you begin to hear what the caterwauling was like when all the crazies at Noddfa started up. But during a rare lull, when all the shearwaters had flown away, my mother's aspirated notes could command wonder. Nurses would put down their urine pans. Rapt inmates would listen as if to the sound of a pin dropping.

She had never whistled before, not that I remember. And she hardly sang either, only in chapel, where the only real audience was the woman standing next to you. In Gerazim my mother stood next to a woman called Hetty who was as deaf as a post, which left my mother just singing to God. She did so with gusto – that entire back catalogue of dirgeful Methodist hits – which collectively assembled more Welsh rhymes than you'd countenance for words such as redemption and pity. Imagine trying to find a rhyme for *anuwioldeb*. Her favourite hymn was '*Wele'n Sefyll Rhwng y Myrtwydd*,' not least because it had been written by a woman. She liked the emptiness in the tune, the chasmic space between the notes. And she liked the simple language, homilies expressed in a minor key.

Before the whistling started there'd been a severe decline in her ability to express herself through words. Syntax splintered. Grammar was wrestled out of shape. Order dismantled. Day by day she lost the world. And she was also spatially confused. When my aunt went to see her she alleged she was in Russia and her descriptions of St. Petersburg's Nevski Prospekt – that grand thoroughfare's busy acts of caretaking and commerce – were as vivid as a marionette show, until you remembered that the old woman had never been there. She had been to Bulgaria once, on a package holiday, but that would only explain a certain foreignness of vision.

When does a person die in your mind? When his or her name is finally forgotten, flashing away like a trout upriver or when you have no recall of a single moment you shared together? No single moment. I cannot pinpoint when things really started to go awry for her, when her world was cut loose like a balloon. Maybe the notes in loose scrawl reminding her of things she had to do. Pay gas. Bring keys. Empty cupboard.

I wanted her to find herself a bower, a shaded settlement among dark leaves where she could build a nest of comfort about her, but that wasn't to be.

On the January day I spotted a glaucous gull near the Cardiff heliport, one of the staff from Noddfa phoned me up to tell me that she'd been fighting. It's not a call you expect to have, ever, let me tell you. About your mother, fighting! Some old collier had taken a pop at her in the dining room – an altercation about digestive biscuits apparently – and she had slugged him one on the nose in return. My mother – the biffer, the bopper, the old scrapper. At least she won the bout. That's a new species of pride. The octogenarian pugilist. The woman who nursed me.

If only she could build a nest for herself. If only those chicken bone fingers could gain enough dexterity to start to weave again. She could then gather spiders' webs, from the undusted nooks and arachnid corners of Noddfa and with that gossamer – strong enough to strangulate bluebottles, delicate enough to trap wisps of dew – she could knit-one-purl-one, give shape to her bower. She could line it with the fine grey hair that candy flosses out of her yellowing skull.

A strong nest, that's what she needs. Consider the long-tailed tit, that busy grey and pink denizen of the willow world. It builds a nest made of moss, hair feathers and silvery threads of gossamer which it shapes into a gourd, strong enough to hold the weight of two birds, and then more eggs, in fact as many as sixteen eggs, and then the rapidly growing chicks and finally the fledgling birds. The whole extraordinary architecture – shaped using as many as two thousand feathers – lasts just the length of a season and then falls apart as if it's never been. So my mother's nest could be one of gossamer, and she could sit contentedly within its silvery threads. Snug as eggs. Her eyes are meshed with red flecks, like a jackdaw's egg.

It took me until I was a fully-grown man, somewhere in my early forties, before I could tell my mother I loved her. I'd visit her every week, without fail, and would take her shopping to the Carmarthen Safeway before it became Morrisons where she would display all the parsimonious skills of someone who lived through a World War, finding every discount sticker and always taking the newest yoghurt pots from the back of the display. We'd always stop for lunch on the way back home in a village so off the beaten track it probably had werewolves scouting round the refuse bins at night. It was in a sharp sided cwm, which never saw daylight, exacerbated by swathes of Sitka spruce that had been planted twenty years ago and now seemed to lay siege to the place. The old lady would eat an enormous mixed grill of chops, eggs and kidneys with all the avidity of a gannet downing mackerel.

The next time I visit Noddfa someone has installed double-glazing over her eyes, and poured liquid cement down her ear canal. She is a shop window dummy and a very sad display at that. Like a down-at-heel florists' showing a wilted tulip in a vase of green water. Zombification doesn't suit her one jot. It's all a matter of meds. You'd have thought that the mighty pharmaceutical industry with its concrete acres of laboratories and infinite profit horizons could devise something to take an old gal's anxiety away without buggering up her locomotive functions. But there doesn't seem to be a magic pill to stop her fretting, to control her hallucinations. One experimental concoction, a mix of chemical stun gun and elephant tranquilliser, knocked her clean into a mini-coma for five days.

I know this guy, Billy Wired down in Burry Port, who claims to have tried every drug in the world: injected ketamine between his toes, snorted peyote in such quantity that he became a pterodactyl for four days and subsisted on nothing more than the occasional Mesozoic fish. He once tried a narcotic from New Guinea that turned his skin permanently green. Even now his skin has a sickly hue. So my guess is that Billy would be able to rustle up something to banish all her anxiety. But at the moment she's at the mercy of the rattling pill trolley in the care home, doomed to a whirling world of hallucinations so powerful that, were I still a drug-hungry student with a penchant for nightly brain alterations, I'd be more than mildly envious of her – someone who could conjure up visions at will, like a starving saint in a cave.

One day Alaw believed a gang had kidnapped her two sons. They had them gagged and bound in the coalhouse and there was dark muttering about being inventive about the torture. Another day she took a sled out over the pack ice to where prowling polar bears scouted for seal cubs, but she could explain little of this, only rounding her lips into a perfect 'O' and making the sound of a tiny hiss. Then, one day, her mind was just one enormous rapture, as colours danced in kaleidoscopic choreography: lilac, diesel blue, mango-green shimmying with powder grey, pea green melding with black of night, aquamarine melting into sunflower and milky cream, and, more luminous than the others, queen of the dance, a shimmering titanium white, executing some dazzling disco to the strobe of her own liquid skin. Billy Wired would have envied her the brain-cinema.

The day we met the consultant at Brynmeillion hospital was a day of cheery weather, with a pearl sun in a Mediterranean blue sky. When he showed us the scan results I thought immediately of tetrads, those kilometer squares I used when mapping breeding birds, from greenshank, spotted by satellite in the Flow Country, to buzzards pinpointed in the Cornish countryside. Spots on the charts marked strokes she's had. The consultant held the sheets as if they were on fire.

'Do you understand?' he asked her.

'Does she understand?' he asked me, noting the vacancy of her stare.

I looked at her head – the fine nose and the blood flecked eyes. Despite her growing confusion these past months there had been nothing to intimate this moment. This demented moment. What goes through that imploding mind?

On a willow wand, serenading the settling dusk, the nightingale pens its solitary symphony. Its liquid voice is a rivulet of delight. But in her nun's room, stripped of decoration, Mam's eyes are wide with fear. They are coming for her. They will get her for certain. She knows. Her birdlike body is a cocoon of tightening feathers, as invisible wires pull her ribcage together, close to bursting point.

In a country she has never seen, the cancer-sickened President has ordered a meal for his penultimate night at the helm. He wants to taste guilt, and it comes in the shape of *l'ortolan*, the bright little bunting. *Emberiza hortulana*, to give it its Latin name.

The birds have been trapped deep in the south of this cruel country by men with lime sticks and near-invisible nets made of horsehair string. They were then blinded in keeping with centuries of tradition and kept in a small bamboo box for a month where they were fed a steady supply of figs, millet and grapes. The ortolan. The fig pecker. When the fig pecker has grown to four times its normal size it is drowned in Armagnac. Steeped to death.

The gluttonous President is also having oysters, *foie gras* and capons but the tongue's great prize is the tiny bird. The erstwhile President tucks his bib into his tight collar, and despite his illness he begins to salivate like a puppy. He then covers his head with a white cloth as the small birds are placed in the oven. A priest with a penchant for finches and catamites started this gourmet tradition long centuries ago as a way of masking his disgusting gluttony from God, away from divine reprimand.

'Father, forgive me for I have eaten everything in the Ark apart from the tortoiseshell...'

The cook, called Fabien, busies himself with the diminutive main course. He reads his notes, because this is an uncommon meal and it is for the President. 'Place in oven at incinerating temperature for four or five minutes. *L'ortolan* should be served immediately; it is meant to be so hot that you must rest it on your tongue while inhaling rapidly through your mouth. This cools the bird, but its real purpose is to force you to release the tiny cascade of ambrosial fat.' Sounds tricky, thinks Fabien, who likes Indian food himself. Especially chicken vindaloo.

Under his shroud Francois Maurice Adrien Marie Mitterrand, the first socialist president of the Fifth Republic, places the entire four-ounce bird into his mouth, its head jutting pathetically between his lips. He bites off the marble-sized head and discards it on the salver provided. It will amuse the cat. He tries to savour his memory of an historic role as the first president for two full terms, his mouth full of bird-body. He knows the rules of history: how they will try to besmirch his name. Not that he thought of that when it came to Rwanda, or blowing up the Rainbow Warrior, or dealing arms to Iran, or running wiretaps or keeping his fig-pecker in his pants.

'When cool, begin to chew. It should take about fifteen minutes to work your way through the breast and wings, the delicately crackling bones, and on to the inner organs.'

Tonight this is the loneliest table in the world, even though there are guests aplenty and an animated chatter resounding throughout the dining room. But at the head of the table is the President, marooned on a glacier of self pity.

He can taste the bird's entire life as he chews in the clouded light: the sibilant wheat fields in the shadows of the Atlas mountains, the salt 'n' seaweed tang of the Mediterranean air, the warm draughts of lavender and pear scent blown by a mistral over Provence and on to the Loire. The pulpy lips and time-stained teeth crunch down with a guillotine certainty toward the pea-sized lungs and heart, thoroughly saturated with liqueur. The tiny organs burst with a sherbet fizz. Quiet, the President is masticating! Listen to the crunch of bird bone. Listen to his loneliness.

Tomorrow is his last night as tour guide of the lost republic and tomorrow he will taste nightingale. Fabien has been given this special request. His men, slinky hunters, assured of success, are already deep in the green woods. They will bring him one, trussed in a net. With this much notice they were lucky to get one.

Fabien, brilliant in his kitchen habitat, will know what to do. He remembers his grandmother and her macabre lullabies:

'Lark's tongue in aspic, thrush in a pie, all the birds that ever sang, sing better as they die...'

The songbird's last serenade will be as short as a gasp. In the kitchen, a man will strop his knife on the whetstone. It will glint, as if alive. He will enjoin his *sous* chef to start a suitable sauce, let it simmer overnight. Let the flavours meld and intensify.

Wild eyed on a twig, the songbird cannot so much as blow a thin note, such is its fear. The hunters' boots crackle like fire through the dry understory. They are pacing out what remains of her terrified life. She knew they were coming, with all of her heart.

White Out

It was the time when an avalanche tore through Rhydycu and Arllen-Fawr, scattering winter hares before it, their fleeing muscles turning missiles, thrown snowballs of terror. They raced to escape the white waves that came pounding down behind them. It went razing Golfa and Ysgwennant, tearing down the walls of farms – Cyrchynan and Bedwan, Cwrt Hir and Tan-y-Ffridd as if they were made of papier maché. It licked cleanly over the land with a Serbian ferocity, gathering impetus from the banks of wind-packed snow ledges behind the sheep folds. Tearing apart Y Gloig, Merllwyn Gwyn and Pentre Llawen with all the certainty of daisy cutter bombs.

What had been snug homes, with dogs at the hearth and Aga, roosters fluffing up feathers in outhouses and babies gurgling, now lay as a fractured syntax of slates and dislocated stones at the valley bottom.

ainw Gsgc wdy w o y e a nchn fa yn n natn y mntr egree pllwnl oyyl brle Wgegn wap

It would take months to tally the death toll as emergency services were stretched to capacity. The Berwyn avalanche was only one incident among thousands. Towns and cities were denied water as reservoirs turned into plate ice and roads were buried under drifts a couple of storeys deep. Some families suffocated in picture postcard settings.

It was a winter beyond imagination.

Pearce lived above the avalanche line. His house stood in the lee of five Scots pines which broke the wind into skeetering channels of air. He had been gathering up the last sheep he could find – maybe a third of the seven hundred odd he had taken up from the hafod only three months before. He fashioned makeshift pens by running lengths of plastic fence between two rocky outcrops. He almost had to mine his way towards them to get them out from the snow and into the gulley where they could be fed cake. He was a sapper again, using trenching tools to excavate his way towards his Passchendaele brethren. The resigned animals waited, freezing. As Pearce burrowed in towards a paralysed ewe, he heard a fantastic cracking sound as the weight of snow half a mile away broke loose from the stratum that cocooned so much of the high hills. It sounded like an overture to apocalypse.

On one of his rare visits to the south – on one of his rare visits anywhere – the old farmer had visited an open cast mine, seen the determined ballet of hundred-ton trucks as they climbed the snail's horn route out of the big hole. Explosives ripped the skin off the earth – the farmed land resembling a Bolivian tin mine.

But this was a sound that made industrial explosives dwindle to firecrackers. He imagined the worst.

He made rude snowshoes by tying wood from old orange boxes onto his boots and walked towards the lip of the land, where the drifts had fallen away into space. He edged his toes forward, a clown on a rope, foolhardy. He was as a child with fire, impossibly magnetised.

It was all gone – six or seven farms – all the livestock, the hawthorn hedges; the very surface of the land had been swept away, the avalanche having stripped bracken and subsoil, ledge and crevice, road and ffridd with it – leaving a landscape bare as the moon. His heart juddered, as if some animal was trapped in his ribcage. There he was, with his ridiculous shoes on his feet and a lamentation forming on his lips as he mouthed the names of all his neighbours. The light was fading. Half past three on a December day. Pearce shuffled back to the farm, his breath laboured as it strained to take in air. Tomorrow he would go down there.

His sleep that night was punctuated by vivid dreams. Etched faces from chance meetings, high on the hills. Pryderi with his nonsense and love of foxes, or the dribble of a congregation at Gerazim, when maybe five or six souls would dust off some flakes of melody as they offered up hymns of supplication to a God that only one of them believed in for sure. And that was Pearce, who in the time left to him would ruminate about the why and wherefore of his being spared. He had nights of visitations – the dead coming to chide him and share a story just as they would on mart day:

Old Bess with her dust cloth cap and her eyes pinched into sharpness above a ferret face, Howard One-Eye and Mog, the wondrous old fellow who still had a horse as a bedfellow in his stable loft bed and a way with his Welsh words that lit up as extraordinary poetry.

By morning a veritable procession of the dead had passed through the cold cell of Pearce's bedroom, a ghastly gang who had elbowed their way into his mind. It was also an inventory, the ones he had to look for in the aftermath.

Pearce pushed open the door of Blaen-helfa to clamber up onto the snowfield and teeter his way for a few yards. The smooth surface was surprisingly easy to walk on, compacted now by the settling and sculpting action of whipping gales. He felt like a giant, striding across the asthmatic land on platform soles. He skirted the path of the avalanche and headed for the bank of birches where the snow was only a few feet deep, deflected by the trees into the corries underneath. The day was gagged by the cold.

Pearce got beneath the tree line and walked on, his legs like insect-stalks as he relearned yesterday's trick of walking on the crystalline surface. He emptied some wizened crab apples from his pocket and set them as bait next to some fishing-line snares.

It took him over an hour to get to Bess' farm, feeling the animal pulse inside him again. Only half of the house was still standing, sectioned like one of those dolls' houses that reveal their interiors. He took off his clumsy snow-shoes, and still went through the front door even though the front wall had collapsed.

It was an act of stupid propriety.

Overnight frost had mummified the room, like sugar dusting the old settle and the cases of stuffed animals. He barked out the woman's name, willing her to appear but his voice broke against the shell of the house. Bess? Bess!

Pearce climbed up the staircase, which in places ran alongside the breach in the wall and called out again, but there was nothing. He felt useless, a stupid old man looking for a body. In her bedroom, with its petrified quilt and enormous leather-bound Bible, he sat down, his breath smoking. He remembered how he had hated this woman. A visceral hatred.

Her father, who everyone called Mistar, had been Pearce's childhood joy – a man who would sit him down on the settle next to the fire and tell him outrageous stories – some true, some fanciful. Pearce loved nothing more than looking deep into the flames, to where the blue gas crept over the coal to ignite percussively and set off fanciful wonders. The old man's voice could quieten to a murmur when he told his tales.

When he was fourteen Mistar had run away to sea, had gone all the way to Kamchatka in Siberia, and when he returned he had run his own one-man coal-mine, with a tunnel that went under the estuary. Mistar told tales of outsmarting the keepers on Maenllwyd estate, bringing home braces of pheasants, woodcock and entire coveys of partridge tied onto his belt. As the old man grew older so Pearce took to looking after him, even after the onset of incontinence which robbed the old man of dignity. And then one day Pearce came to visit him and he had again soiled himself, but this time his wife had smeared the shit across the old man's face and he was sitting there, too weak to move, too weak to remove the yellow smears of runny excrement. Pearce went to get a knife from the kitchen and he would have killed her, there and then, he really would, but morality bound his hands together, held him back.

Later that evening, as he carried the old man's frail frame to bed in the next room, he took hold of the pillow and would have smothered him, put him out of his misery and humiliation, and he would have done it but the wires bit into his flesh again, telling him it wasn't right. That night he learned all he would ever need to know about love and hatred and from that day on he began to see things in black and white, so that he either loved something or hated it and there was no grey place in between. Life was clearer that way.

Having checked every remnant of a room, Pearce had to conclude that the old lady was buried under the rubble. Leaving behind the shambles of stone he felt the old lady walking behind him, an after-breath of life. He reached the farms along the ridges, some under heavy blankets of snow, all ruckled now into jagged sheets that were unreachable. The ravens would have their first brood before the men came up from the town, a dozen of them, on a JCB, the yellow machine groaning as it tried to bank the snow onto the sides of the main road.

At the next farm there was nothing other than a

cloying silence, and around him the dead shapes of perished stock. The father, Steve, lay with his head mulched by a falling beam, a dark stain around the eye that faced Pearce. The other three bodies were corralled on the floor around Steve, as if they had moved towards him as a place of safety. His wife, Florence, was frozen in an impossible position, with both hands pulled far behind her back. The children lay at the base of Steve's chair, one hugging each foot. 'Bring your little children unto me' was what it said in the Bible, but Pearce now knew that Jesus didn't love them. The poor children had pain-wracked faces, taken aback by the absence of angels they'd been promised.

Pearce decided to sleep that night in the barn. The outbuilding seemed to have deflected the ferocity of snow. When he pushed open the door he heard a little whimper, almost human in the way it affected him.

'Who's there?' he asked, peering into the darkness. He could hear the creature holding its breath, willing the very bellows of its lungs to miss a few beats.

'Is there anybody there?' A wounded whimper.

Pearce could make out a pair of eyes, which blinked shut as he strained to make out what framed them. Then he heard a voice.

'Gawje?'

A word which triggered very old memories.

'Y-y-yes,' he said. 'I am gawje.' Not gipsy. He hadn't spoken Romany for half a century. He never heard it since the horse fairs stopped.

'My name is Pearce,' he said, stretching out a hand.

‘Eiza.’ A thin voice.

Pearce remembered that he had some biscuits in his pocket. Reaching into his coat for them caused the girl to cower back into the corner.

‘It’s alright,’ said Pearce, his voice dropping down through the registers until it reached the pitch he used when reassuring trapped lambs. He showed her the packet. She moved slowly towards him. She took the biscuits and began to pulverise them between her teeth. Pearce hunkered down and rolled a cigarette. The lighter flame shed light on the child.

She was fourteen or fifteen and dressed in two or three coats which had seen much better days. But she was luminously beautiful and even though she was cold and scared she had a haughtiness about her, the eyes of an Andalucian flamenco dancer. The girl was mad with the business of the biscuits.

‘Is that better?’ he asked as she wiped her mouth with her sleeve. Her eyes sparkled with hunger.

‘How long have you been here?’

And then she told him all about her wanderings, ever since her mother and father had been taken away from her and she had found herself travelling byways and green lanes, crossing moors under moonlight, learning to live off her wits and a flair for spotting nature’s gifts. Autumn had been a feast of chestnuts, hazelnuts and berries beyond measure. She had gathered baskets of fungi and sold some of them at farms on the high hills. But the weather, when it turned, had been her undoing.

Peace was amazed that he could understand her.

He'd heard Romany many times as a child but had no idea he carried so much with him.

'What happened to your parents?'

She turned her head away, scrutinising the wall as if it told secrets. He let the subject drop and suggested they should start walking back to his farm where she could spend the night, and have some soup. She fixed him with an accipitrine stare.

They walked into the gloaming. The land was preternaturally still and the only sound was their breathing. They were plumed by vapour as their exhalations fogged in the chill. It seemed a long way now and Pearce's joints protested as they clambered over the tops of smothered trees. There were snowlamps hanging in the sky, a wintry candelabra about to be extinguished at day's end.

The girl marched on, buoyed up by thoughts of the broth that was promised. The old man had promised leeks and carrots. Pearce struggled to keep up, his breathing shallow now. She asked him questions with every step, a trick to keep them going, give extra purpose to their strides.

'How old are you?'

'Who will pluck the birds – you or me?'

'The dead people – who were they?'

'How many carrots?'

They had called by the snares on their way and all five had taken, a total of two fieldfares and three redwings. Eiza took one of the thrushes from Pearce's hand and scrutinised it, appreciating the beauty of its plumage and weighing up how much it had to contribute to their supper. He looked at her, a halo of refracted light throwing her black hair into stark relief and rimming her eager, scanning eyes. He thought he's never seen anyone or anything as beautiful in the whole span of his days. He took her hand in his and kissed it, his back creaking audibly, so that they both laughed and there was no embarrassment. Pearce saw the shadows gathering, and was aware, for one terrible and heavy moment, of all the love he might have encountered had he not lived his lonely life with only a dog to converse with and the small talk of wind in the eaves. Eiza looked up at him and smiled.

'We should press on, before it gets too dark.'

The moon made the hills incandesce, a snowy phosphorescence. It took an hour longer than he thought it would. The map of the land was almost without feature.

Pearce lifted the latch of the door and ushered Eiza inside. She took bold steps ahead of him into the bare room. In the chair was the old farmer's body, his glazed eyes like trout on a slab. He must have been dead for some time.

You never know how it will come. It might come as a young girl, or as a raven, or like the tolling of a bell where there is no bell, or even a steeple to bear it. One thing is sure. To see the rumpled pile of human clothing you leave behind isn't easy. Ask old Pearce, as he trudges off into the snowfields, leaving behind the gipsy girl plucking her pile of winter thrushes.

Shearwater Nights

It was a summer of sex and seabirds, arranged around two events that were to shape Kenny's life forever. He would always remember that bright season, full of sea campion, the coruscating light of the tide-race, inquisitive seals and mewing seagulls, which ended with an extraordinary meal, fit for a Queen.

Kenny had been sent to the island because of what his docket sheet described as 'transgressive' behaviour. A docket sheet was written by a probation officer before a court appearance and was in part character survey, in part character assassination. They were duty bound to declare everything about him that was bad, but the good bits were added at their discretion. In Kenny's case the docket was like giving permission to line him up for execution by machine-gun fire. There was something about Kenny that poisoned his probation officer's bloodstream and set fire to his clothes. So when Kenny was had up for three burglaries he thought he'd be in for a long stretch. In the judicial system crimes against the person were as nothing to jemmying into an Englishman's home, being his castle and all that. Those were really punished.

Luckily the judge in court was a bit more benign. The probation officer saw a villain in the making: the judge saw a seventeen-year-old who had made bad decisions. Kenny's docket said he was interested in nature, so the judge suggested that he serve a long community sentence 'somewhere with a bit of nature.' So they'd found him a job as an assistant warden on Bardsey island, a few miles off the spike of land thrown by north Wales towards Wicklow. The community was a bit sparse there as you might expect, being a storm-tossed isle in a wind-tousled sea.

He arrived at night as the boatmen were forced to wait for the wind to die down and the tide to turn. The boat powered through a silver lake of water which corralled the moonlight and even gathered light from the stars. Its surface was pixelatedby far off constellations.

He'd spent the afternoon killing time in a sharp-sided cove on a crash course in island lore. The boatman Wil Rogers knew the waters hereabouts like the back of his hand, which would make them tobacco-coloured with nicotine reefs, judging by the smoke-scale that had built up as far as Wil's gnarled knuckles. Wil told tales of treasure and pilgrimage and astonishing finds after shipwrecks, including a cargo of rare wines which washed up case after case for a month or more. The lighthouse keepers drank their fill of Chateau La Tour that summer.

At night the island was a hump of rock set in scintillations of water. The boatman aimed for the calm waters of the Cafn, a harbour dynamited into existence by Trinity House engineers in the Fifties. As Wil's hands tilled the craft to shore, concentric rings of moonlit water rippled away from the oars.

The lighthouse was automated and the farmed land was tended by a family who actually lived on the mainland. There was no permanent populace. Centuries of pilgrim visitors had been replaced by holidaymakers who revered the deep quality of silence and by birdwatchers who twitched at the sight of rarities, such as the exceptional marooned migrant, a gray-cheeked thrush which landed after a westerly. It looked like bugger-all to any non-birders, but actually had people chartering helicopters to see it, despite the risky power of October storms. And autumn had those alright, when the sea could change from pewter mirror through churning green to waves like witches' hats in the time it took for a seal to yawn.

The warden, Ryan Teale, met them between the small stone ridges of the harbour, bellowing out a hearty welcome as they hoved into land. His foghorn voice resonated on the rocks, unsettling some oystercatchers that were roosting on stands of kelp. Ryan had gone to work on Bardsey straight after completing his diploma in Countryside Management and appreciated the distance it put between him and his head-banging family. His father was a heroin addict and his mother a loose woman. Had there been a remoter posting he'd have taken it, the Isle of Mull or Fair Isle maybe? He'd also left a fevered affair with Mathilde, his lecturer in animal husbandry, a woman with summer-fruit lips, who was married to the principal of the college. To never taste the raspberry flesh again, to bite it hard in the maelstrom of fervid sex was like a prison sentence for him. But her husband had found out, and he was a member of skeet team and so had a gun. Scarpering like a coward was the only option and Ryan took it.

'You're Kenny, right?'

'I am that.'

'Good to have you here. I think you'll like it more than prison,' Which got that subject out of the way.

As they walked up the only track on the island, referred to fondly as the A1, Kenny heard his first shearwaters. When he'd first read about them he'd thought it was almost worth being branded a career burglar if he could spend time on an island with an enormous colony of shearwaters. They seemed like emblems of wilderness and freedom as they traversed huge oceans on outstretched wings.

He was staying in Cristin, an old house which might have been home to any one of a dozen Daphne de Maurier heroines. It had windows with driftwood mullions separating the panes of thick glass. Kenny shared a bunk bed with the other assistant called Twm who was out doing some work, even though it was one o' clock in the morning.

'Don't expect to get too much sleep this summer. There's work to do by day and night, but anyway you're a young bloke and won't need too much sleep,' said Teale, without any ill-feeling.

They were all three up early to catch some birds for ringing. They unfurled the mist nets and set them between bamboo poles in the withy beds where they would trap birds in pockets of netting. While they waited for some birds to be caught they walked to the shore. Light was widening as a line above the horizon. Small birds, willow warblers and a few whinchats, flitted among topiaries of gorse, sculpted into dense, contorted thickets by the prevailing wind. There had been a significant 'fall' of birds overnight, determined migrants which had been blown off course, attracted by the light, fluttered pathetically to the ground at the base of the lighthouse.

The three men walked to the shore and shared a thermos of coffee above the cove called Solfach. The pulsing flashes of the lighthouse dimmed in effect as the sun rose in the east, ballooning slowly over the peaks of Snowdonia and the ridgebacks of Yr Eifl, Pegwn Nebo and Mynydd Rhiw.

Twenty minutes later they visited the nets and all of them had caught: all in all some ten species of passerines, including a beautiful male redstart, in a livery of black, grey and red, which Kenny thought was one of the most beautiful things he'd ever seen in his life.

Ryan deftly unfurled the birds from the pockets of net into which they'd settled and popped them into canvas bags to carry them back to the ringing room in one of the Cristin outbuildings. There Kenny was shown how to measure the wings and weigh the small birds in small plastic cones clipped to weighing balances. They noted the abrasion on the wings, which helped age them, and then attached the tiny aluminium rings on their legs, gently squeezing each one closed before releasing the captive bird into the safety of one of the fuchsia bushes.

Once he'd been shown how to process a morning's worth of catch, Kenny was told he could do the following day's rounds himself. He was also taken through his other duties including earning a place on the rota for emptying the chemical latrines. The other assistant, Twm, offered him a clothes peg to cut off his sense of smell in busy visitor weeks. Twm was a funny man. Had a bag of clothes pegs, too.

The days passed as a series of reveries for Kenny who was lost in the delight of the place. It was a mad swirl of sense and experience. The tang of seaweed reminded him of the iodine his mother would put on cuts. He was given two lobster pots for his own use, which he placed in the protected waters of the Cafn. Favourites, above all else, were the whirling nights when shearwaters claimed the air above the island. Cocklolly, they screamed. Cocklolly! Whipping through like tiny gusts. Nothing that happened by day could compete with the joys of shearwatering. The birds gathered offshore in roosts on the water, waiting for the safety of darkness to settle. Kenny studied them. On land they were ungainly, their legs set far back so that they could barely manage a brief waddle into the safety of their nesting holes. At night they ran a gauntlet of great black-backed gulls which stood sentinel at the nest entrances, eager to guzzle down the little petrels, bite sized snacks for the voracious, powerful birds. In the morning the island was littered with the remains of these feasts – sternum bones picked clean of flesh attached to the indigestible bird parts: the feet and wings. As if supplying a soundtrack for these vicious meals, the shearwater cries were bloodcurdling. In the dark they were the banshee wails of disembodied spirits.

'Those cries are what kept the Vikings from landing on the Calf of Man,' said Ryan as he picked up one of the birds to ring it. 'They were in their longboats ready to seize the island at night when they heard all these voices as they headed there, imagining them to be the ghosts of long drowned sailors and they decided not to claim this cemetery of a place and carried on further south.'

One afternoon they were walking past Sister Briony's house when they both saw something terrible. Sister Briony was a nun who lived alone in a house called Tyddyn Non and devoted much of her time to keeping the holy wells on the island open. One almost always saw her carrying a First World War trenching tool.

'Fucking hell, she's crucified herself!' said Ryan, pointing to where the old woman was pinioned up against the window. Go down there and I'll go to telephone for help.'

Kenny had rushed down to the house and shoulder-barged his way in, only to find her naked in a tin bath, caught in mid act as she sluiced down some water on her back from a small tin pail. She'd washed her habit and hung it up to dry in the window. Flustered, Kenny made some embarrassed noises and retreated, carefully closing the door behind him. He ran as fast as he could back to Cristin where he just managed to stop Ryan calling up the air ambulance as he was making the connection on the radio telephone.

The next time Kenny saw Sister Briony he averted his eyes, but she strode purposefully towards him and said in her feathery voice:

'It's alright,' which was a double shock as Kenny thought she represented a silent order. 'It's alright.'

As summer unfurled along with the fronds of verdant bracken Kenny really took to Twm's company. He was fearless and funny and Kenny loved their climbing trips across to the steeper side of the island where they counted seabird nests. Twm, for his part, loved Kenny's tales of being in a street gang. Kenny told one in which his best friend was deliberately blinded.

One afternoon they found an old tennis ball washed up on the shore and Kenny cut it in half, ready to show Twm how to open the central locking on a car by placing it over the lock and hitting it hard. Another sultry day they wormed their way into a cave where they came eye to eye with an enormous bull seal, which snorted its annoyance, an interruption to its dreams of unending mackerel shoals.

When they took a break from their seabird surveying, Twm would untwine a fishing line and send a weighted, baited hook out into the waves. As if he were a conjurer it would be no time at all before he hauled in two thrashing pollack. It was a trick he could repeat with consummate ease, getting up a rhythm of deftly placing the bait in the water and then pulling the fish out. He used mackerel tails as lure, pollack attracting mackerel but never pollack to attract pollack. It was all a tad too cannibalistic.

They would often return from these expeditions garlanded with fish, which they'd barter with visitors to the observatory who would often swap something tasty in return. They got apple pies, tinned stuff, tobacco sometimes. Once they got a whole wedding cake, which had its own story.

Before each and every climbing trip Ryan proved his worth by checking all their climbing kit with an attentive eye. He checked the carabineers and tugged at key lengths of rope. He was their guardian for these months, and he proved it.

At the beginning of August Ifor Magnus, the farmer who worked the island during the summer, asked the three men if they could help him with some tasks, bringing in the hay and rounding up the sheep. Haymaking was a trip back in time. They worked alongside some of the holidaymakers, under a burning sun, until their muscles wilted. After they finished every last bale and piled them high on the back of the tractor-trailer, Ifor and his wife Petula slaked their thirsts with flagon after flagon of delicious perry which had been left to cool in one of the deepest wells.

It was as much as they could do to get up the next day, let alone form a human cordon around the island and walk in tandem rounding up sheep. All of the visitors helped with this task. All the visitors, even the ones with young children, worked the flat parts of the island while the observatory staff worked the sides of the mountain over Talcen Mynydd and Briw Gerrig.

It was cooler than the day before but Twm and Kenny still pumped sweat as they climbed over the scree and followed precarious sheep routes. It took three hours to get the sheep down to the pens near the harbour and from there it was just a short operation to get them into the yellow Second World War landing craft that would transport them. Ifor asked if Kenny and Twm would be happy to come over to the mainland to help him disgorge the animals. Ryan gave his blessing and the lads beamed.

The craft was low in the water as they left Y Cafn, chugging along under great plumes of diesel smoke, past Trwyn y Fynwent, Traeth Ffynnon and Pen Cristin. The sequestered animals were restless and fidgety and Kenny and Twm kept out of the way by hunkering down in the corner and smoking roll-your-owns despite the thin spray that drenched everything in the boat. Then, with a rolling movement that seemed to throw all the animals to one side, a freak wave threatened to overturn the craft. A mighty ram, bellowing hoarsely with fear, scrabbled to get over the side and it coincided with the craft being low in the water. Over went the animal. Kenny only just managed to get his hands to its fleece but as the animal's pelt absorbed seawater it became lethally heavy and pulled Kenny in behind it. The shock and force of the water took his breath away. The ram bellowed once more in fear before it sunk towards the lobsters. It all happened so swiftly but as the waters carried him away at five knots, away from a landing craft that was itself chugging away from him towards Aberdaron at a rate of some five knots, he still felt naked terror. He felt himself diminish out of sight as the cold of the water tore into his torso.

Twm raised the alarm and the craft turned slowly. Kenny was learning to tread water for life itself. The craft, with its cargo of agitated animals, ploughed against cross currents to gain on the bobbing form of the lad. He was losing the fight now and he could hear voices from his past mixing with the surge of the water. He bobbed under, once, twice, the salt water alive with desire, wanting to fill up his lungs like balloons. When they got close enough Ifor snagged him with a fishing gaff he normally reserved for bringing in tope. It was only afterward that the old bugger confided that he could easily have decapitated Kenny as he swung the big shark hook towards his shoulders. Luckily it caught in his shirt collar and, by dint of the two men heaving with all their might, they pulled him in and upwards so he could catch hold of the tires draped along the hull. Kenny vomited over an ewe and, as they turned once more for Porth Meudwy and the white houses of Aberdaron, he kept on vomiting. He had never liked sheep.

August meandered to a close in a flurry of squalls and dramatic storms with fork lightning spearing the sea like tridents. Ryan had gone on a busman's holiday to do some bird-watching on the Coto Donana and had left his two assistants in charge. They only had a couple of visitors staying in Cristin for the last week of the month and they were two Californian girls, called

Karen and Sharon. They were glamorous stoners, so laid back they were almost laid out, smoking pot all day right up to the point in the evening when everyone convened in the Observatory to compile the species log for the day.

Kenny and Twm were astonished they managed to remember who they were or where they were, let alone amass the impressive tally. The girls found a woodchat shrike and an icterine warbler in the same bush: an avian double whammy.

Twm and Kenny were pleased beyond measure to see them both, as they were both new species for them. That they were spotted by two attractive young women – taking a year out before heading for prestigious universities – was a bonus. The four of them flirted outrageously and for Kenny, who had never been anywhere further than Carlisle, Karen and Sharon were as exotic as shrikes. Karen made Kenny's heart speed up. She had eyes that flashed with wickedness and merriment and he loved her fit body with tanned legs and lithe thighs. But the lasses were only booked in for a week. On the day they left in the Good Shepherd, Kenny felt a pang of hollowness. He would miss Karen's smile and the green tang of Moroccan hashish that trailed behind her everywhere. Just before she left the island he'd teased her to be careful going through customs in Aberdaron. For a fraction of a second she believed him, which made the two of them laugh. Kenny watched the boat diminish to vanishing point. He'd hoped for a kiss.

The weather harshened and blustered throughout

September. But with the inclemency of the weather came astonishing night-time spectacles as birds in their thousands were attracted to the lighthouse beams. Floodlights illuminated a patch of ground near the base of the lighthouse designed to stop birds pulverising themselves against the glass and in most weathers it worked. But when the storms whipped in or a cloying mist swirled around the light the birds would sometimes just fly straight in to the glass and brain themselves, falling stunned to shiver and die at the base of the structure.

It also attracted more rare birds to the island. One night it attracted a river warbler, which wasn't much to look at but Kenny remembered it was one of the things Karen was most eager to see. Kenny asked Ryan if he could ring her with the news. When he spoke to her on the radio telephone he could swear that she was as pleased to talk to him as he was to speak to her. They left it that she would try to cadge a lift with the helicopter that was bringing Trinity House engineers out to clean the light. Kenny hoped the little skulking bird would stay, or survive that long.

When the helicopter landed on the pad in the lee of the lighthouse the two girls were on board, laughing uproariously because they'd just been told a ribald joke by the pilot. Ryan was the one who suggested having a dinner to welcome their guests and bid farewell to the island after more than a few hefty tokes of Moroccan head scrambler which the girls had passed round in an ornate hookah. He suggested they all have a grand dinner the next night, cook up some of the birds that had fallen to ground the previous evening.

In the meantime they tried to relocate the warbler, which required all their skills. As it transpired the bird was in the observatory garden and they all saw it before breakfast. It really wasn't much to look at, but it had travelled a very long way to pick late midges around the fuchsias.

The warden had been up since dawn and had taken two bin sacks with him to pick up bird bodies at the base of the light. He also took a big gunney sack for the big bird, which was to be his surprise ingredient. It could have been a dinner depicted by the brush of an Old Master: watchers and two engineers, sitting in the light of the Tilley paraffin lamps, surrounded by various dead birds. They had a starter of lightly grilled breast meats from redwings, so fat with Russian berries that it was as if they'd already been marinaded with redcurrants. They then had game birds – two woodcock, four snipes and a redshank – barbecued outside by Ryan, who handed round a bottle of sloe gin which they all drank out of observatory mugs.

They say Richard the Lionheart was the first to bring the mute swan to Britain, one of the spoils of the Crusades. It was the biggest bird ever to fly into Bardsey light and Ryan had done well to hide it from his diners and to squeeze it in to the oven. As he presented the dish, to a spontaneous burst of delighted applause, Ryan told them how the only person who was officially allowed to eat swan was the Queen, but reasoned that no-one on the island was afraid to break protocol. The Trinity House guys had loved the redwing starters and the thoroughly smoked wader-kebabs. The youngsters couldn't give a hoot.

To make the two American visitors actually feel like royalty Ryan had made cardboard crowns which they wore to great effect, causing all the dinner guests to guffaw at the way they donned them at rakish angles. Sharon said the swan looked liked the biggest thanksgiving turkey they had ever seen . It took up most of the table and even then its long neck lolled over one edge. A warm miasma of conversation had settled in, and they were all heady with the effects of drink.

'Shall I carve?' asked Kenny, running the blade of a carving knife against a whetstone. Twm had suggested he do the honours as he was the one with the knife skills, an in-joke based on some of the stories Kenny'd told him about gang life, and about the way they sometimes duelled with Kitchen Devils. Ryan was now on his feet.

'By Royal command, I give my subjects consent to eat a mute swan. And have some potatoes while you're at it.'

Kenny looked at Twm and at Karen as if he was torn between which of them warranted the most of his love, but as he chewed on the breast meat of the enormous bird he knew that he had enough to go around. Twm excused himself as he needed to pack his stuff while he was still able to think – he'd swigged back the sloe gin as if there was no tomorrow and was more than slightly befuddled from the drugs. The flesh of the stately bird was plentiful, if tough, and the remaining diners munched through it doggedly.

Taking the air outside Kenny and Karen listened to the plaintive sound of the last of the summer's shearwaters. *Cocklolly,* it cried as it wheeled over the island in the dark before turning its elegant wings for Uruguay, to shear its way across the tempestuous South Atlantic. *Cocklolly,* said the spirit guide, departing. Kenny knew he could find his own way home now. His hands interlaced with Karen's, his eyes straining to see the retreating bird in the absorbent dark. The world contracted to the warmth of her hand and it was more than sufficient. And in the fuchsia bush the little warbler slept on as the light flashed out its steady semaphore. Keep away. Keep away. Keep away.

Too Cold for Snow

In these northern latitudes Fahrenheit zero was considered bikini weather. It is the coldest inhabited place on earth. It was said that one old man had stopped walking for a moment one afternoon and the blood had frozen in his veins. The Eveny, a migratory people, therefore had every reason to keep walking and, besides, they were just keeping pace with the animals. Hovki, the God, made everything around them, but details of how he did this are vague. After all, it was a long time ago, but they do know they belong to all this, all that's around them and to nature, as if it's a cousin. Their word for bear is the same as grandfather. And they have been here long enough to know that the elders fly to the sun on the back of the reindeer.

The animals lumbered across the moss, its sphagnum coverlet wrapping up all sound. Little bamboo rods of sunlight pointed the way among the endless thickets of birch which made the taiga seem uncrossable. The reindeer herders were hunchbacked by the weight of the cold, which had scattered splintery ice on the bundled layers of hide and pelt which cocooned them all from air which had most of the effects of liquid nitrogen. And trudging with the animals at five miles a day was Boz, who had come all the way to the lung-shattering temperatures of Siberia to avoid his wife.

It was more a question of avoiding his wife's vindictive brood of a family who had vowed, with a vehemence bordering on the vibrant lust of Albanian blood feud, that they'd never forgive him for leaving her in the lurch. Their collective memory was selective enough to forget that she was the one who had run off with the manager of the Smiling Kebab. The Smiling Kebab, for fuck's sake!

Boz was a composer of advertising jingles and he now lived with nomads the other side of the Verkhoyansk Mountains. They wore seventeen layers of clothing in winter, but he wore eighteen, just to be on the safe side. He hasn't thought of a ditty for months because he saw a reindeer killed by a stab to the base of the skull. Odd how life seemed like a straight road but then showed its switchbacks. His mother-in-law scorned his music – said he'd been educated beyond his intellect. She could make him wither with shame. So he was fleeing two women, at least.

The rhythm of walking was conducive to thought, and the genus of Siberian plodding in harsh midwinter was one most richly so. One tread. Two treads. One tread more. An action so mechanical it gave you time to think about things, as the reindeer cloaked you in a fog of frozen breath.

Boz thought about his wife and Len McLaren –

the two deserved one another. Anyone who could be seduced by a man who had kebab lamb fat under his fingernails deserved to be indecently and unhygienically palped by them. The thought of the man's hands on her flesh had first made him sick, then incendiary with rage before being spirited away into the dark place. Boz took to drink awhile as if he could afford to do so. If tequila is the fuel of incipient loopiness then he supped his fill, downing it as if Mexicans were smuggling it across the Brecon Beacons on mule trains, or in petrol tankers. But every so often someone would unkindly mention how his wife's cartoon-hellish family, the Thompsons, were plotting their revenge – how they were going to watch him burn as he dangled from a home made gibbet. In some ways the Thompsons were inventive. It was a family to avoid. That and their gibbet.

In rare blazes of sobriety he thought of dramatic ways to escape his plight, even considering a stint with the French foreign legion until Mel, the barmaid with a zoo of animal tattoos told him that: 'It's fantasy island for hard gay men, who like their castles in the sand.' She could be ever so dismissive – Mel, who had been educated at the Sorbonne, but had discovered crack courtesy of a spiral-eyed Moroccan at Jim Morrison's grave and had lost her way through great swathes of Europe courtesy of amazing hallucinogens and hospital-grade cocaine. It was her who had showed him the advert in the *Western Mail* from a Galway based television company that was looking for a Welsh speaker with high stamina and a rare sense of adventure to spend a year with the Eveny, a reindeer-herding people who take their stock back and fore across Siberia. One of their ancient tracks was about to be severed by the creation of an enormous pipeline. Last Migration of the Eveny, as they said in the *Radio Times*.

He took the idea seriously and before he went for his interview he gave up the sauce and climbed up Twmbarlwm twice a day until his calf muscles resembled those of a Bolivian gaucho in the Altiplano. He cashed in his Premium bonds, sold his car and exchanged all the money for a lift in an old Soviet helicopter, a deal brokered by some vodka-jowled businessmen who looked as if they got their suits from a boutique called Mafia 'R' Us.

The helicopter took off from a military airfield littered with broken Antonov planes, rusted relics of an Empire that only lasted seventy years. It was a sepia scene from some Cold War film or other, especially as the ice mist smothered everything. The flight took for ever, especially as they had to stop for 'mail' every now and then, landing on airstrips that looked no bigger than a cricketing crease where there was never so much as a letter to deliver or to pick up. On the other hand they did drop off cases of booze and picked up animal pelts, but he knew better than to ask a why or a wherefore. The captain had some words of broken English. His breath was a miasma of caries and slivovitz and he stabbed a Cumberland sausage finger to emphasise each triumphant word.

'You...'

'Yes, me...' said Boz, smiling with all the fake

encouragement he could muster, realising that this was the man entrusted with his life once the rotors turned. And that he'd had more than a drop of booze.

'You, you like?'

'Yes, very much.'

'What you like?'

'Very fine helicopter. Sturdy and solidly built. And you, well you are an expert captain. All those birches to avoid. And you do so, effortlessly.'

'What sign?'

'What sign?'

'What sign you?'

'What sign?'

'I, Capricorn.'

'Oh star sign, you mean? Me, Virgo.'

'Is good luck?'

'I believe so?'

'You need it where you go.'

With that the captain took his ursine frame up to the front end, whatever that was called in a chopper, leaving Boz to digest the frozen puddle of fear which had settled in the pit of his stomach. Was Capricorn meant to get on with Virgo? Could the Captain see that they only managed to clear the tree canopy by the breadth of a squirrel tail?

Boz had known better trips. In fact he'd rather cross Hades with his ex-wife than hear the grinding of the rotors, which sounded as if they were, well, rusty, though now oiled in a ghastly way. Yes, he'd rather run through hell in a gasoline suit, swear to God. He thought of his mother, a woman he had learned to love very late – strong, impossibly talkative and proud of him whatever he did. Love he was leaving behind.

It took another eighteen hours and two vertiginous landings before they reached the rendezvous point. It was pitch black, a quality of blackness that Boz had only experienced once before in his life when his grandmother had locked him into the cupboard under the stairs to punish him for stealing ginger beer.

The Siberian stars were obscured and the moon was all darkside. As they bundled him and his bags outside he felt certain that they would wait until morning before taking off, but with an alacrity that would have taken his breath away were it not for the fact that the cold had already done just that, the chopper and its crew left him there, the captain's face a demonic green glow in the reflected light from the instrument panels. They had dumped him off in the middle of Siberia, with only a thermos to keep him warm.

But with a snuffling sound they had come, the ten families and their hundreds of animals, with not a word of Russian or English between them, just gentle words of Eveny, a language that sounded as if it were made of moss. The Eveny. Whose time was almost over. As he filmed their four mile trudge each day, their breaths leaving a skein of mist hanging in the air, Boz realised that this was history in the making, a nomadic pathway about to be severed. He remembered the time he had seen grey whales heading north to Alaska, following ancient tracks in the sea with no other impulse other than to cleave the waters with their bulk, hoovering up plankton and jellyfish as they went, and with only the skittering auklets to keep them company.

Reindeer meat, dried like pemmican, was the staple food. But there was reindeer milk, and in the night fermented reindeer milk, served from sacks that must have been intestines at one time. Although this strange beer was tainted with hairs and passed from lips that had never known a toothbrush, there was something effortlessly comforting about the slow effect of the alcohol and the accompanying susurration of beasts encamped outside their tents, and the occasional smile of the children who were wrapped in so many layers of fur that glimpsing so much as an eye was an achievement.

At each camp you fed the fire with vodka to placate the evil spirits. One evil spirit for another, thought Boz. They burned mountain rhododendron which gave off a sublime smell. And in a new tent, with fresh larch branches on the floor and reindeer hides weighted with stones around the back and sides of the tent, the mingling of heavy aromas was enough to wrestle you to the ground. The reindeer bells made Boz think of yachts as they warned off the wolves.

Each day was a repeat of the one before, the brash of tiny birch twigs snapping underfoot, the pantomime observances of trying to pee in sub zero air. He'd read too many stories about Arctic explorers taking off their socks and a couple of toes peeling with them. Boz passed water as if it were a timed sport. In this universe, cold is the unending, basic condition. Heat is a luxury, a temporary flicker. Keep on moving.

They had been walking a week. Once they passed

a cliff that had been sheared open by a deluge to reveal nearly intact mammoths – the animals that first scooped up river mud with their tusks to form dry land. Boz was due a delivery of batteries which the chopper was going to drop near an oil well marked as a black gush on the map. It was one of only three features on the homemade map which the helicopter captain had drawn him for a price. There was also a military installation that was marked with a gun and a small hillock which was a geological mystery.

For the herders his maps were idiotic. They didn't have any fixed points in their entire world view, so they would relate everything to their movement through a place. *Dyu* was the present camp site but only a destination for a moment before it turns into home and the starting point for the next migration and so three words would follow each other over and over again – *amdip, duy, erimken* – previous site, present site, next site – *amdip, duy, erimken* – a triad of movement.

But even though they were in the right place on the right day the helicopter didn't show. With a mild sense of panic gripping his bowels, Boz decided to walk along the wire perimeter of the oil installation, but it seemed to go on for ever and Boz noted with a sinking feeling that the filming might be over. As he might be over, at least the Welshman who left his wife and ran away with the reindeer might be a done chapter. If the chopper didn't find him, his life as it had been lived was over too. Soon it would be winter, and the days would barely exist. He would be marooned with people he couldn't call friends because he didn't even know the name for friend in their language, but for whom he cared deeply, because of the simplicity of their lives, the doggedness of their journeys and the chinkling chimes of their children's laughter. These were kids who didn't have so much as a single toy between them and yet they played constantly. He ate marmot with them and so much reindeer meat that he was almost permanently constipated. One day he sighed with relief when they mentioned sausages until he found out they were made with reindeer blood in a skin of intestine.

And then one day he saved a little girl from drowning. No-one said thank you and her mother received her sodden body with no tears or even a shrug. But something happened. Acceptance happened. He watched them slathering bear fat on her wounds where her ribs had struck some rocks before walking out to see the men rounding up the animals for castration.

A flash of silver caught his eye and he could see what looked like a small bulldozer making its way across a snowfield towards the fence. The reindeer herders froze. This was another sight that wasn't budgeted for in their cosmologies.

In a land which had never had a Renaissance, and where science first came in the form of an airplane which had buzzed low over the treetops with its cargo of cartographers, geologists and one anthropologist, even the fence was an original. Metal was unknown to them, all their tools, everything they had came from their animals – trenching tools from the antlers, water carriers from the innards, even jewellery, after a fashion, made from carved hoof and tiny stretched strips of hide.

And here, in their party, was Boz, the man who wrote songs to sell lingerie and Belgian chocolate. Who once lost his cool because a company said he couldn't overdub a ukulele on a twenty second blurt of noisy rubbish. Boz with his camera, trying to make sense of this way of life, which seemed to have elevated dignity and unfathomable wells of sadness.

Beyond the fence, Boz watched the twenty-first century stuttering towards them, with a huge man squeezed into the Lilliputian cab of a mini bulldozer as if he was never meant to ever get out of it. Through the fiercely frosted pane of the cab the man was smoking, as if the pinprick glow at the end of his cigarette would keep him warm despite the plunging temperature drop. The fug of smoke and the obvious contortions of his enormous frame as he roboted the gears made him look inhuman. They all watched the little bulldozer come to a halt and were mesmerised by the spectacle of the man pouring his flesh out of the cab like toothpaste coming out of a tube.

The man walked up to the fence and there was a long silence as they absorbed the sight of him and he evaluated the look of Boz and his Trappist clan. After a few minutes the man rasped out some questions in Russian and a young Nenet stepped forward to translate.

'Who is he?' said the Russian, his hands flopping dismissively in Boz's direction.

'He is a man who is working a film for us. He came in the air.'

The other herders shook their heads in agreement even though they didn't have a clue what they were on about. Behind them a bull reindeer snorted as if he was taking umbrage.

The Russian nodded pensively.

'Is there anything he needs?'

The young man looked at Boz, showing his palms in what was near enough a universal gesture.

Boz saw the fork in the path before him. The one that saw him playing cards while he waited for the oil company transit to take him away and the other path, where he stayed with his friends and completed the journey and only then worried about how the hell he'd get home. He could wait for a clattering helicopter to take him the hell out. Or stay here with a people who had survived atom bombs, uranium mines, bears, enforced work at the Bolshoi Nimnir gulag and the *khitry* wolves. Even if the vodka might get them in the end.

He knew which path to take, into a place heavy with the ammoniac tang of reindeer piss, and where the night's duvet of warmth was his snuggled up neighbours' bodies, every one of them snoring as if they were worked by bellows, and the morning's weak light was an ineffable triumph beyond the skills of any painter to record. Just as certainly as the lead reindeer, the *hunyuk,* sets the pace like a shaman with a drum he knew the path he would take. *Amdip, duy, erimken.* It led into the unknown, which to him was now curiously familiar, as familiar as his old mother's face, smiling at him through the birch trees, proud, after all this time, of her wandering son.

TV Land

The sun might someday set over this place in tropical glory, a spaghetti of tangerine light slivers and sauvignon ribbons looped into the west. But not quite yet, not while there's more grey rain to fall. Not in this city of bad teeth, sodden litter, mangled dreams and three skyscrapers. Don't come here if you want New York's irrepressible verticality. Or neon retina fizzes from an advertising frenzy like Tokyo, or L.A. chunky smog, or the sheer teemingness of Kampala. Some cities you measure in epiphanies: this one you measure with a stick.

Let's spin around the cardinal points. To the east the Great Suburbs of TV Saturation. To the north it's all Georgian and Edwardian mansions set in jungly leafiness, alive with blackbirds. Old money, deep roots. To the west a garden village gone to seed and, to the south, where the river used to meet the sea, they've closed the river mouth, that spastic act. Mosquitoes activate here, loving the septic lagoon.

This random city.

In a church a priest auditions new choristers with

a tear of lust in his eye. They sing Bach and a piece by Arwel Hughes which conjures up pictures of snow.

A Somali boy, ten years old, recites great tracts of an oral literature passed on generationally. He will learn them all, he thinks, the tales and the poems and give them to his children in turn. He is an extraordinary librarian.

In a house in Canton a man wonders how on earth he came to buy a three storey house without any stairs. There's just a big hole and a rope, thick as a naval hawser. To get to his own bathroom he has to climb like an orangutan and his hands have rusty calluses.

Three hundred thousand stories like these, random and signifying. The life of a city.

On one street, north of the bus depot, a yellow burger van stands on a bleached-out street, doing a roaring trade. Marty Sathyre smirks demonically as he counts out the change. The punters who dine at his upmarket burger van would never guess what was really in their free range guinea fowl baguettes. They'd gag if they did.

He'd been out early with the traps – set them in an avenue of decaying trees behind the bakery – where collared doves and venereal town pigeons with club feet foraged and fought over the grain that slipped between lorry and silo. It took him just over an hour to fill a small sack, despatching each of the birds with a Victorian police truncheon he'd boosted from an antiques market – along with a badger hair shaving brush and an ivory handled nose-hair trimmer.

Marty's long-time girlfriend Poppaline hated all

this butchery and went on and on about it so much that Marty even thought of giving her the heave-ho, and would have done were it not for her trampolining carnal skills.

His brother helped him pluck the birds and then roast them, giving them an extra ten minutes in the hot oven 'just in case of disease.'

The kitchen table was sticky with gizzards and innards. Marty's hands looked like psychotic glove puppets due to the dozens of small feathers stuck there. He washed them in Swarfega, then looked up the recipe for a Peruvian dish called *cuy*, then phoned his mate Iorwerth to line up the ingredients. Marty didn't just confine himself to cooking disease-riddled town pigeons. Oh no, his was cooking fit for an epidemiologist.

There's a popular Quechuan folk song, sung by tribes on the high altiplano. 'Hey old lady' goes the rhyme, 'you're as ancient as the Andes, as fickle as the wind, and if you want me as a son-in law open the door and cook some *cuy*, whole *cuy*, mind.' And then the song turns into a call and response, 'The door, the door,' sung in a subsonic, Richard Burton voice and then the words 'the *cuy*, the whole one' in a castrato's falsetto. It's a song of gender ping-pong.

The doorbell chimes, one of those comedy numbers with a recording of a football commentary describing a Cardiff City goal.

'Iorrie, how's it hanging?'

'Could be better. Pam's left me. Said she's moving to Norwich.'

'Norwich. Jesus. Fenland. A place where a man can be his own first cousin. That is serious. I'm so sorry but maybe I can take your mind off things? You still fit for a spot of hunting and gathering?'

'If I really have to.'

'Get me two dozen if you can.'

'Surely.'

Iorrie, under a cloud of misery, gathered his stuff and drove the van down to the end of the street, hung a left and pulled over. He pulled on a pair of heavy waders over his jeans, put a substantial rubber torch in his waterproof jacket, put up the portable cordon around the manhole cover, then, in one move, prised it open and lowered himself down. The water gurgled with ordure.

He'd gotten used to the smell of the sewers years ago. In fact he suspected he'd lost the sense of smell altogether when Pam had mentioned the fragrance of night-scented stock wafting out of the garden one August night and Iorrie couldn't smell a thing.

The inky water swirled and sloshed around the Victorian brickwork as he made his way to the traps. He'd bought them on the internet, from an industrial estate in Vietnam. Air freighted in three days. Best fifty quid he'd spent in a long while. Best rat traps in the world and when he heard the manic squealing he knew he'd be able to service the order fully. Marty must be cooking fake cuy, he thought, as he opened the mouth of his body bag and reached down for the first to die.

A quick neck break is the best means of despatch. In Ecuador they press the small head forwards for a painless quick death and it retains the blood in the body, a big fat tic wrapped in a hairy duvet. Throat cutting is frowned upon as it leaves the meat dry.

Cuy is a pretty adaptable ingredient. Broiled or boiled. Fry one after first hammering the meat as if you mean it, exacting revenge on it, beating seven kinds of merry hell out of the flat escalopes of flesh.

Make a broth if you fancy, use snow melt from Ubinas and herbs only the old women in the market know about. Create a consommé so thin it looks like dew. Taste it with a precious spoon. A silver *cuy* spoon from Potosi.

Meanwhile, in one of the northern suburbs of the city, a man was waking up. He was Marty's nemesis, and their paths were soon to cross.

He'd known rough mornings-after-the-night-before but nothing like this. Not one where he ended up with a human foot in the sink. A bloody foot in a bloody sock in the fucking sink. Brennan stood there, transfixed by the stump, with the sheer anatomy lesson of it, the veins, the dangling tendons. He dry retched, then splashed his face with water. He had the mother of all hangovers which required a high cholesterol breakfast. Food helped him think, nursed him through the occasional crisis. And this was a crisis. Brennan thought there was nothing like a good pan full of fat to get him on his feet again. Kidneys. Hash browns. Cumberland sausages, plump with the wrong sort of fats. The biggest looked like a big toe. Which brought him back to the foot again. It wasn't going to simply walk away. He would have to do something about it.

But not without fortifying himself with another bacon bap. He owed himself that much at least.

Where had he been the night before? He must have gone to the Green Parrot, because he always went there at the start of a bender. It was always Happy Hour down the Parrot, giveaway prices for cocktails. He'd had a Scrum Five, without the grenadine. (His mother had once told him that pomegranates were the devil's own fruit so you'd do well to steer clear of them.) After that he'd gone down the Meat Quarter, to goose some biff, but the biff wasn't what you might call easy pickings. There was an octogenarian disco-queen in a PVC top, her breasts squashed like fried eggs in the strobe lights. She danced as if a surgeon had removed the part of her brain responsible for co-ordination. And there was a scar, just beneath her hairline, which looked as if it was the place the neurosurgeon had tried to push left-over matter back in.

Brennan downed a few pills. He'd bought them from The Lizard, a man with skin like a crocodile handbag. Born on a toxic waste dump, that sort of complexion. There was a pink and white one and a sort of buff-coloured one. He took them both, not feeling in the mood for careful experiment, more in a wanton mood. He took to the dance floor, avoiding eye contact with the go-goer, lest she ensnare him in that familiar plot which would result in a kneetrembler in the bogs. Maybe they'd been temporary lovers in the past? He couldn't remember.

The DJ was transporting the dance floor to Ibiza. A girl was swinging her head in time to the strobe lights. Tiny droplets of sweat sprayed off her hair, an electric mist.

The pills kicked in quick and loving warmth coursed through the cartography of his veins. The nightclub walls closed in on him, vectoring him back into the womb. He felt snug in his own skin. It was during the next twelve-inch club-mix of some saccharine-laden eighties disco shite that he passed out. Brennan had no recollection of what happened to him. Alien abduction, maybe? With Bolivian cosmonauts, in aluminium foil suits. One thing was certain: he had a foot as a souvenir.

When Brennan left his flat, with the foot neatly wrapped and carried in an Adidas bag, Muggs was waiting for him. Muggs worked for Luther, the head of Cardiff's mafia, known jokingly by some as the Taffia. Brennan knew better. Knew them to be hard as marble and bereft of scruple.

'Put your foot in it?' asked Muggs.

That fazed Brennan, mixed up his brain mash.

'It's a fine day. Let's walk.'

Luther was poolside at the house with a peroxide floozy called Tristar having just applied a lot of her lipstick to his joystick. He was still flushed by his minor exertions, fussily pulling up his trousers

'Take a seat Mr. Brennan. Can we offer you a drink. Maybe you could do with something after last night's visit to the horror shop.'

'I can't remember what happened last night.'

'We filmed it all, don't worry: the chair, the power tools, close ups and cutaways. We followed all the basic rules of film grammar.'

Brennan hated overeducated thugs. Give him old school, no school.

'Me? I did it? Did what?'

'Well, we filmed someone who looked like you, setting about this poor man with all the righteous fury of a Jeremiah. Do you want to see?'

Brennan shook his head. The creature that brought him bad luck was there in the haze, the amphetamine genie run amok.

'So let's talk turkey. Marty. He's the one who's brought us together. He is costing me a lot of money. My vans and shops aren't selling shit all at the moment. And for every new van he puts on the streets I'm taking one off. Well, enough is enough. The deal is this. I want Marty's imperium to end. Do that and your life will turn once more on a well-oiled axis. With me?'

Luther was infamous for his fleet of vans, serving what the locals referred to as "death kebabs", offering a salivating choice between shish made of condemned meat and doner made of abattoir off cuts: pigs' lips and arseholes, left over gristle, bloody floor-sweepings. Many people woke up on Sunday mornings with caves of limpid fat where their mouths used to be.

Brennan had no choice. Luther was an evil serpent, but this was a rocky path to be walked unshod. He liked Marty, respected the man's ingenuity, his naked gift of scam. And the scale of his audacity. Like that time he sold tarmac and offered a special mix of marble which would make the owner's drive stand proud in a long street of driveways. It would cost a bit more, mind. After they'd laid it the effect of the white chips 'from a family run quarry outside Turin' against the jet black of the mac was striking. He'd shaken hands, and packed the lorry. Come the first rain the Polo mints they'd thrown in the mix would melt and the drive would become a pockmarked mess.

Or the bootlegging. Marty captured some of the all-time best gigs on his miniature recording equipment, made on the sly by his cousin Wilf who worked in a M.O.D lab somewhere near Aberdeen. He was the first to release Brian Wilson's *Smile*, that work of dark symphonic majesty which, had it come out before the Beatles' *Sergeant Pepper*, would have made the Fab Four look like the Muppets they really were.

Two months flew by at an amphetamine lick as Brennan made his plans.

Meanwhile Marty's success bred more success. He bought fifteen more vans with a grant from the Welsh Development Agency – scamsters themselves in shiny suits. He had the coolest of logos designed by Pete Fowler, the guy who does the Super Furry Animals' artwork. It was a dining dragon, the creature resplendent in a white tuxedo and quite the apogee of monster sophistication. And over a round of Warsteiners in Chapter bar his friends brain-stormed a logo for him.

'Enter the Dragon.'

'Too Chinese.'

'Or perverse.'

'What about Marty's Mess, like they have on ships?'

'Or Perfect Taste?'

'I like that.'

And so was born the slogan that would wrap around the base of the dragon's tail. A Chinese dragon breathes water and is fertile, making crops grow. A Welsh dragon spits flames fit to chargrill a quarter pounder. This one had those words curled up to sit on.

Demand threatened to outstrip supply, and with a profit margin that made even the bloated one that fast food normally commands look quite anorexic against the four hundred per cent mark up at P.T's. It was worth creating a small team who would trap underground and venture up the valleys to catch wood pigeons, carrion crows and rooks. They paid a farmer called Steve a lavish retainer for keeping quiet and laying the corn in stubble fields where they would use rocket-powered nets to capture a flock at a time.

The menu expanded.

'Perfect Taste'

Grilled spatchcock burgers (collared doves collared behind the bakery – same weight as a spatchcock only a damn sight cheaper) £4.00
Guinea fowl with grape foliage (woodpigeons by another name) £3.50
Wild rabbit with organic green leaf (sewer kill mainly and kids were paid by the carrier bag to collect dandelions) £4.50

They sited the vans near office blocks at lunch time, drove to events in four counties, even went to agricultural shows where no one asked so much as a question. Lips were smacked. Taste buds were tantalised. They raked it in off the vans. One made eight grand in five days. There was a bad incident one night when a bunch of yobs overturned a van which caught fire and the man inside, Terry Fetch, only just managed to clamber out through the hatch with his life. He was lit up like a magnesium flare, screaming like a banshee, his clothes burning into his dermis. A Samaritan yob who hadn't legged it rolled the flames out with a coat and then scarpered. Marty paid for the plastic surgery, jokingly offering to make him look like Robbie Williams, but Terry never smiled after that night, wasn't able to really, not with the way they had to reconfigure his jaw. That was the only shadow on what seemed like a perfectly sunlit and profitable summer.

It was an October afternoon when a television researcher rang Marty to ask him whether he'd like to be a guest on *The Johnnie Smooth Chat Show*. Marty said yes. He'd never been on TV and he liked Johnnie Smooth, his ready banter and punishing asides. 'You're as welcome as syph,' was one of catchphrases, this self-crowned 'King of the Putdown.'

The velveteen-voiced honey ended the chat with Marty: 'Next Thursday, live on air at seven, so you'll need to be at the studio by half past five if that's all right, for some make up and a quick run through? We'll send a cab for you to the house, yes?'

'I look forward to it, Melissa.'

Melissa was on Brennan's payroll now. As was Johnnie, although his help depended on morality rather than money, convinced by Brennan that what he was about to do was for the public good.

The make-up lady was a doll and the researcher, Melissa, was a doll and the producer of the programme, Henry, was a gushing London queen slumming it in regional television after an accident during the making of a documentary at the British Museum, when he'd insisted on getting a better angle on a Ming vase which he nudged off the table. The crew and the mortified curator seemed to count the minutes before it hit the floor.

'May I say,' simpered Henry, who would have made a good Beatrice or Delilah, tottering on heels, 'that I think your burgers are ravishing. Quite the best this side of the Atlantic and you could even give them a run for their money Stateside. Ever thought of franchising over there?'

Marty hadn't until Henry put up the idea and he squirrelled it away. He knew that people lived in the sewers in New York which might be an advantage, or maybe not, and he knew that they'd hunted down the passenger pigeon – once the most numerous bird on earth – until there was just one left, shuffling off a porch in San Diego zoo, a ten inch drop to extinction.

'Let's take you to meet the man,' said Henry.

They went through a labyrinth of corridors until they reached a door marked with an enormous star, with dozens of thin strips of gold fanning out from its centre.

They knocked and entered.

'Come in! Come in! Care for a blueberry margarita. Heaps of vitamin C. Let me tell you Marty, I do admire your products. Very much.'

'Have you ever tried any?' ventured Marty with a certain bitterness. His hackles were up because Johnnie addressed him via the mirror, not deigning to turn around.

'My researcher brought in a wild leveret thing which tasted pretty divine. You've got some good products and I hear Mammon's looking after you well.'

'Mammon?

'The false God.'

'I know who Mammon is, but what are you trying to imply?'

'Nothing, chum. Look, don't get in a tizz. Don't get my stage persona mixed up with the fifty-two-year-old-bloke who's been on the roller-coaster. I've seen ups and I've seen downs and at the moment I'm having a drink to settle my nerves before delivering verbal bad ju-ju to the nation. Why don't you? People get nervous under the television lights. We had to give one contributor, a taxidermist from Prestatyn, a cup of tea laced with Mogadon before we could get him on the set. Trouble was he'd had a few slugs from a hip flask apparently and we only just managed to stop him attempting fake coitus with a stuffed leopard he'd brought in. On air, mind! In front of all those people.'

'I'll have what you're having.'

'And if we're talking about gods,' said Johnnie, 'these are their faces.' He pointed to what seemed like a mini-shrine in the corner, a four foot high block of cork to which were attached a collection of men's faces.

'These are the tabloid men, the ones who make and break people like me. *Daily Star*, *Mirror* and most pungently, *The Sun*. And here's my favourite headline from that august organ. The Institute for Strategic Studies wanted a pacifist, a token pacifist to join their board and they invited Michael Foot because he was just about the most famous one around at the time – even though Bruce Kent was probably the pacifists' pacifist – and he accepted. The *Sun* ran it under the headline 'Foot Heads Arms Body.' Marty was laughing as he sipped his powerful margarita.

In the technical area the floor manager was saying his mantras, learned from a wise man in a tree house in Kerala.

'The water lapping the mangrove roots is the sound of a safe place, is the rhythm of home.'

He took a deep breath and walked into studio D to do the warm-up routine, the usual limp-as-lettuce gags followed by the health and safety drill. On air in ten.

The director in the gallery looked at his watch. Almost an hour before he could get to a bar and shaft a lager and maybe, if his luck was in, pull one of the impressionable little vixens who worked in accounts. The production assistant sitting next to him was wondering if the small wager she'd had with Camera 4 would pay off. She'd predicted that tonight was the night Johnnie's show would drop off the ratings graph. This run had been getting worse and worse and they simply weren't getting the names. In this celebrity age, that was the kiss of death. And talking to a guy who flipped burgers for a living wasn't exactly *Big Brother* in Buck House now was it? Melissa had told her this show might be better than she could imagine.

Precocious bitch. All that Oxbridge la-dee-dah!

The audience was a blue rinse brigade from some Women's Institute up the valleys, who found Johnnie as shocking as the advent of menopause. It was always some Women's Institute from up the valleys who arrived in buses that had seen better days.. They had to pay them to come, calling it a subsidy for the bus when in reality they were paying a tenner a head to fill the seats. There was also a smattering of younger folk who came of their own volition because they liked the scabrous humour of the host.

The resident band, with its vertically-challenged musical director Billy Sharp struck up the familiar tune, marred somewhat by the fact that the trumpeter coughed during the middle eight, making a sound like some German sound terrorists.

The floor manager counted down and in he walked, down the glass stairs with the fur-lined banisters in a zebra striped suit with pink chunky-heeled winkle-pickers, and did that mince of his that made him a gay icon to rival the Beverley sisters, all three of them. The biddies hooted and yollered, the youngsters bayed in appreciation.

'Glamorous people, a good night and the warmest of welcomes to the show of shows. And if your name happens to Graham Norton: go pinch other people's ideas, you bag of spent fuck.'

The audience went off like a firecracker, fake shock and real shock. For the TV audience the expletives would be bleeped out by a nimble-fingered vision mixer. It was all a part of living on the edge.

A crash of snare drums. Marty appeared in a backlit window to the side of the stairs. He forced a smile through his mask of pinking embarrassment.

'And tonight we have for you a self made man, a man of means, not a mean man. His name is Marty Sathyre and he's the King Farouk of fast food, the top cat of takeaway and a genuine burgher of this town. More from him later but we start, where Billy?' Spinning round to where his MD was just climbing down from his conductor's wooden box.

'I don't fucking know ya knobhead.' Said for the crowd's sake. They loved insubordination.

'So what have you got there. What are you eating on the sly?'

'Shortbread.'

The audience went off on one. They loved the predictability of the dwarf jokes – the 'shortarse slot' as some called it. He dismissed Billy with a hand gesture and looked at Camera 3.

'Who wants to come up here and try their luck with Johnnie?'

Three quarters of the audience had their hands up, but tonight they weren't choosing at random. Dirk was a plant, there to add spice to Marty's night of TV hell.

The steadicam operator tracked him from his seat to his place in front of Johnnie's throne.

'And you are?'

'Dirk.'

'Not the most charming name but nevertheless you are the chosen one. Now kneel and kiss my winkle-picker.'

Dirk did as he was told. Week on week they all did. After all there was a holiday in Rio hanging on the next few minutes.

'What do you do when you're not feeding on the bottom, or maybe it's some man's bottom. Ych a fi, what an image. I'll need electroshock to expunge that image out of my head, you parting a pair of clenchies with your fat little tongue.'

Dirk stood up.

'So what tiresome little job do you do Dirk?'

'I'm a-a-a-trading standards officer.'

'A s-s-s-tammering standard trading officer. Bet you do well at public speaking...'

'No, it's trading standards.'

'I know what it is you smug-brained fucking yokel. Hit that button vision mixer Meg, keep us on air, why don't you?'

Meg would resign after tonight. It was ridiculous what she had to go through, what with the Head of Programmes saying it would be her fault if any Anglo-Saxon swearwords were accidentally aired.

'What do you do exactly?'

'I'm working on a case of food fraud.'

'Would that be fast food coz if it is you might like to meet my main guest. Stick around for him.'

The light came up behind Marty's head but this time he looked quizzical, a tremor of nerves animating his lower lip, so that he looked as if he was on the verge of saying something.

'Anyway let's see what the viewer's choice is tonight.' Viewers were invited to send things in for the contestants to taste, blindfold. They were encouraged to send in either something too vile for words or something nice, Samaritan food.

'Let's see, we've got a mouth watering selection of Vomitorium Surprise, Preparation X and Aztec Two Step, each served on doilies handmade by some of the darling ladies of the audience.'

The camera tracked along the third row, where the gleeful ladies were having the times of their lives as Johnnie invited them to join in the chant.

'Choose, choose!'

Dirk's finger hovered over Preparation X (sent in by Mrs D. Roberts of Blaenau Ffestiniog, an apprentice witch of the high slate country). He then pointed at the Aztec Two Step.

'Knife and fork for Dirk, not that you need a knife seeing as a dirk is a small Scottish knife. That would suit you Billy, wouldn't it – a short Scottish knife, you fucking stupid dwarf.' Meg the vision mixer missed that one. There were ructions later on.

Two scantily-clad leggy blondes tottered in on high heels, one bearing a fork and another bearing a knife. Expect the death threats from the feminists, thought Henry.

Dirk ate the food, which after the first moment of imagined revulsion caused no revulsion. In fact it tasted very pleasant.

'What d'ya think, Dirk, darling?'

'V-v-very nice.'

'Is it indeed, Dirk – well we'll find out later what it is you've allowed into your alimentary. Let Kylie and Charlene take you over there to sit down so you can digest things. Dirk, ladies and gentlemen! What a waste of a skin!'

The band played the sting that announced the evening's main guest. The assistant floor managed ushered Marty onto the staircase and he was momentarily dazzled by the lights. He sat down in the chair opposite Johnnie, a seat deliberately upholstered to allow the guest to sink in and look uncomfortable right from the outset.

'Well, Marty. They tell me you're a millionaire, not that you could tell from those clothes.'

'Wah-wah,' went the trumpet, applauding the joke.

'As I said, you're a self-made businessman. Who made you, Doctor Frankenstein?'

A snort of trombone.

Even though Marty was not bad looking he seemed uglier, slumped into the sofa. He also hadn't managed to get a word in yet.

'You've created a small empire of burger vans – top class stuff, haven't you?'

'Yes,' managed the discomfited Marty, who was starting to sweat now. He was aware of a droplet gathering on the tip of his nose.

'So where do the recipes from? Do you steal them from books or are you a naturally inspired chef?'

'I picked them up on my travels.'

'That's not all you picked up I hear. My, my, what an articulate man we have here. Loquacious and erudite too. And where has our well-travelled wordsmith peregrinated in this fair planet?'

'I've b-b-b-been here and there.'

The audience squealed at this embarrassment.

'Ever been to Latin America, Marty, ever ventured there? They eat guinea pigs down there I hear.'

Camera 4 cut to Dirk's face, alert now. Marty was caught like a collared dove.

'Do you know what would be a wicked wheeze with the emphasis on wicked? What if you substituted sewer rats, good old *Rattus Norvegicus* for guinea pigs and served those up on a bap? That would make good business sense wouldn't it? Tell me now, wouldn't it?'

Marty tried to get up but the sofa's capaciousness restrained him.

'Ladies and gentlemen. This man Marty Sathyre does precisely that, serves up rats in burgers, pigeons in kebabs, all manner of unspeakable filth is served up as food and he has the audacity to dress it up as fine provender. Let's bring on Dr. Filigree Watson, an expert on animal pathology.'

A pantomime mad scientist made his entrance, an egg-shell head above the obligatory bow tie.

'You've examined the contents of Mr. Sathyre's products, Dr. Watson. What do you deduce?'

'I have no doubt that the main ingredients on the menu of 'Perfect Taste' include the brown rat, the common wood pigeon, collared doves and some evidence of crow and grey squirrel.'

'But they're not described as such on the menu are they Marty?'

'No, they're not.' And with those words his number was well and truly up. On a cue from the floor manager

Kylie and Charlene wheeled the familiar wooden contraption into place in front of the band area where its members were donning sou-westers and rubber coats.

The audience broke into spontaneous braying.

'The stocks! The stocks!'

Zombified by shame, Marty was led to the stocks where his hands were slotted through the holes and one by one, in a curiously sombre Indian file, the audience members walked up, row by row, to hurl buckets of food-swill at him. Not a frenzy. All controlled to ensure that he was still being drenched as the credits rolled. They intercut shots of Dirk being sick in a huge brown bag.

In a house on the southern rim of the city a priest was watching the box to fill his mind after what had happened after choir practise – another young life besmirched- like wiping an oily rag across an innocent cheek.

Even though he had been warned about the deadening effect of television, a very young Somali was resting awhile after his feats of memory, watching the buckets being hurled, embarrassed that his grasp of English wasn't sufficient to understand all of Johnnie's badinage.

In a house in Canton a man switched off the set and went to piss in a bucket because he didn't have the energy to climb the rope to the bathroom.

As the announcer's voice went into the 'same time next week' spiel, Luther opened a bottle of champagne and punched in the numbers of Brennan's mobile so he could congratulate him for a job well done. His girlfriend Tristar cut a couple of lines of coke, her long, black painted fingernails clacking on the mirror surface like crows' beaks. The Bolivian marching powder was high grade. It would be a night of manacles and sweat.

In his dressing room the star of the show took off his jacket and put it carefully on a hanger. He thought to himself about the wares he peddled, which pulled people together, brought them close. This virtual community in a world going mad. This flickering lamp, lighting the faces of the brain dead, who'll go on watching even as the stars descend and the cities burn. Watch it in widescreen, watch it on plasma screen. Watch it any which way. Johnnie knows.

A Cut Below

Despite a whirling wind which threatened to throw the rugby posts into the air like chopsticks Keiron Lye put in another performance of a lifetime. Yes, another performance of a lifetime, outstripping even his own abundant excellence, in the face of a mid Wales monsoon, where the rain and wind hurled buckets of water into the players' faces. They were drenched in a way more profound than any one of the bedraggled supporters could remember. It was wetter even than that fabled trip to Nantyffyllon where Hughie the prop almost drowned in a ruck when his head was forced down into a huge puddle on the half way line.

Holding his head up as best he could in a wind which wanted to bend his spine into a sickle, Keiron scythed in from the touchline, cutting through the defensive line like heated cheese wire through margarine. There were so many flailing arms reaching for him he felt like a man snorkelling among octopuses. Four very experienced players were made to look like lumbering dolts as he jigged and weaved through the spray. Keiron finally palmed off Resolven's full back, who fell down in an awkward pantomime motion.

There were old men in the crowd who thought they would take their last ever gasp watching Keiron play. He was excitement on legs. Their hearts raced at the mere sight of him. One of them had to clutch his chest cage, so severe was the thrill of one of his tries, catching a grubber kick from one of the centres and making a dummy pass before outflanking three men in a line by running the long way round them, leaving him with a good five clear yards between his touchdown and the nearest trailing opponent. He was a player with southern hemisphere skills: you couldn't laud him with much greater praise. He was good enough to be selected by the All Blacks.

Keiron was the embodiment of rugby skill, powered by huge heart and guts, guided by innate intuition, and blessed with an ability to instantly read a game like a Gareth, Barry or Shane. He easily matched any of the greats and, by now, even this early in his career he almost casually surpassed them. Keiron was wondrous. Keiron was a shift-changer, able to turn from corporeal rugby player to untackleable wraith in a magic breath. An alchemist, too, able to transmute the meatiness of a defence into a whisp of smoke. And he was surely going to be picked for a Welsh cap now that one of their scouts was in the crowd.

Keiron had blazed in Newtown for almost a season but because he didn't play for one of the big sides he was under the radar for a bit, a comet unreported until the local paper started to put him on the front page. Then a BBC reporter churned out a pretty ordinary piece of TV about rising rugby stars, which included some amateur footage of Keiron's coruscatingly good second half try against Nantyffyllon, which despite the rain-which-should-have-stopped-play was a classic. Other badly framed shots recorded his crunching tackles, including upending a sixteen-stone forward and tossing him into the mud like a doll.

His teammates carried him off the pitch at shoulder height. They enjoyed having him in the team. He made them enjoy the game more, gave them power, bestowed, well, virility; even if he himself was disarmingly effete. He'd slathered on all sorts of poncy unguents: patchouli oil content, jasmine scents and you might catch a glimpse of frilly underwear.

Off the pitch he was disarmingly camp in his manner, as 'camp as a row of pink sequin tents' according to one piercing wag. At the start of his first season some of the grizzly old buzzards who'd been playing for the team for years and years took offence at Keiron's lack of manliness. But he won them over on the pitch. As he ran tiny clumps of grass thrown up from his studs sprayed behind him as if he were sowing seeds of future greatness. He chinked. He wove. He was majestic.

One Saturday he single-handedly racked up eighty one points during the course of a heatedly violent game, scoring one try that seemed to defy gravity as he floated over a Resolven player and drifted down like dandelion seed to score. Who else could invoke comparisons with dandelion seeds when he drifted in from the touchline? Or similes involving peregrine falcons when he flew in to make the hard yards? Or have staid commentators suggesting that he ran like a man able to outpace his own shadow. One fan gave him a boot with silver studs. Real silver. No kidding.

There's a drunken panoply of post-match rugby club beer, but among them Keiron was as unexpected as monkey fern orchid growing out of the centre spot. Keiron identified perfumes, singling out individual scents he picked out from the olfactory orgy that was the Saturday night crowd, when the players' wives turned up for the disco. He would name them without shame and with unerring accuracy. Daisy by Marc Jacobs. White Jasmine and Mint Cologne by Jo Malone. Cristalle by Chanel. L'Air Du Temps by Nina Ricci. Stuff by Chloe, Madame X, he'd get it every time. Nail it. He could have made a living out of this ability, found a niche on TV somewhere, as he inhaled deeply and identified which celebrity perfume was on a girl's skin. The players watched him, bemused and impressed as he named each woman's perfume in turn. Mariah Carey, a saddo's down-at-heel and frumpy smell; Christina Aguilera, a seductive little number which proved just how far the girl from Staten Island had come since the days when she appeared on TV on the New Mickey Mouse Club. Keiron knew the back story as well as the most avid reader of *Hello*.

In the air tonight: Christina and Britney and Jennifer Lopez, Gwen Stefani, Paris Hilton and even Sarah Jessica Parker.

The forwards started betting on him getting one wrong. His fellow backs backed him to the hilt, until there was a pot of over three hundred pounds resting on his naming the perfume Mart the butcher's wife was using. It wasn't one he recognized at first. It was expensively vulgar, more skunk than musk.

'It's that new line from Chanel – Gymnopedies, I think,' laying on a laughable Breton onion seller accent as he said it.

And before he could be probed about the actual name Mart blurted out the word 'Gymnopédies' and by then all were roaring with delight, especially as Watkins, the ageing centre, said that the backs had won fair and square but the winnings were all going behind the bar to be drunk with abandon.

'To salve your weary souls, gentlemen,' he said, lifting a pint pot to a tumultuous cheer.

Keiron sat down with his rugby friends and tried to concentrate on what they were saying in their cups amid the din of disco music. But his mind was far away. He was thinking about his forthcoming sex-change operation. In an opulent Harley Street consulting rooms an Australian doctor made absolutely sure he was decided on this course before starting his hormone treatment to enlarge his breasts. The doctor had even taken him out for dinner afterwards. All part of the service.

Keiron wanted to tell them, he really did, but he knew that things would never be the same. They'd probably never want to play the Perfume Challenge with him ever again. And never allow him to disgrace a rugby field. It was one thing to accept his odd ways, it was quite another to play with a girlie.

That year the Six Nations competition started on

October 8th with Wales pitched against their deadly rivals, England. It was an old saw that Wales and England still went to war for eighty minutes. Keiron Lye scored a try which earned a place in the pantheon, shrugging off three tackles, outpacing a full back who was renowned for breakneck speed and doing a ceremonial forward roll before grounding the ball. On the Sunday he went quietly into the clinic for a bilateral orchiectomy where he had both testicles removed.

He'd told the coach he wasn't coming for training on Monday, citing personal reasons. His consultant had told him to rest for six weeks but Keiron, headstrong with pain, ran out for a full session on the Tuesday, even though he might have burst all his stitches. He deftly avoided tackles, gritted his teeth and made damn sure the team doctor didn't get within a diagnostic mile of him.

In the changing room he kept his shorts on and said he was going to shower at home, and no one thought twice about it. Other than the coach, who had noticed how he winced more than once when running, and who had also noted that his running style was less graceful. After three more training sessions he felt obliged to ask Lye what was going on. Keiron was disarmingly frank.

'I'm in the process of changing gender. I've been on hormones for eight months now and during the Christmas break I'm due to have a penectomy...'

'Is that...?'

'It is.'

'Jesus H.'

'And that'll be followed by a vaginoplasty...'

The coach counted to six, a calming device.

'What is that exactly?'

The coach blanched when it was explained to him, and this was a man who'd been with the Territorial Army to Helmand province in Afghanistan, worked in a field hospital where unspeakable injuries came in on convoys and Apache medivacs.

'But the good news is I'll still be able to play.'

The coach bit his lip. He wasn't so sure. He did, however, know he was talking to the greatest player in the history of the game, Keiron Lye, who was already set to eclipse all the significant point scorers; Keiron, who never missed a kick, whatever the angle, who almost always scored once he had the ball in hand. There was an unstoppable force about his running, as if a deity had put on togs. As if a man in a chariot with blades on its wheels was facing an opposition of tulips. He made it look that easy.

The two of them decided that they would have to tell the chairman, then the team and then the world.

The W.R.U. was rugby union's equivalent to an in-growing toenail – old, encrusted and irritating. The emergency board meeting was in state of collective catatonia, especially after the physio started to explain some of the procedures that would change Keiron into a full woman.

Chairman Gwilym Morthwyl Prosser, still drowsy from the previous evening's whisky, managed to bumble to the heart of the matter:

'Is he allowed to play for us, as a woman, that is?'

Charles Eminent, Q.C., had a voice desiccated from his time in ancient European libraries, pursuing his passion for medieval bestiaries. The law, for him, was just a means to an end, a way of bankrolling his time among the strange animals that wandered the corners of old vellum manuscripts.

'It's such an unusual situation that there isn't anything in the statutes at any level,' said Mr Eminent, exhausted from so much legal spade work.

'And will he be, well, equipped for the challenges of the modern game?' asked Prosser, looking for a way out. He always felt like a vole in a room full of buzzards. His were antiquated, reactionary views but he felt he represented the fan in the street. Once upon a time he did, but then came electric light, the dawn of flight and the suffragettes.

Gerry Harthill, the physio, reminded the board that women were stronger in many ways than men.

'And he's growing breasts, I understand?' asked Prosser. 'That will be a distraction, if nothing else.'

'I've discussed that aspect of things with both him and the other players...'

'And...' prompted Prosser.

'They say no one fancies him!'

The laughter dissipated the tension in the room. Not that it was strictly true. One of the second row players had caught himself looking at Keiron a bit too often. Something about his eyes, and the softness of his skin.

The press conference was electrifying. Barely had they got to the substance of the event before one of the shabbier papers sent a cohort of reporters, armed with cheque books, to ferret out lovers, winkle out one night stands of his. But Keiron had been celibate for a long time, and before that he'd had one long term girlfriend who had become a nun. She lived on a holy island and sent him cards at Christmas and Easter that she decorated herself with dried seaweed. Keiron had a fleshy memory of her wearing a basque and wondered what God made of her then.

At the news editors conference at the British Broadcasting Corporation they were having conniptions over who should be covering this most delicate phase of Keiron Lye's transformation. Should it be the Health Correspondent or was this a story for the Chief Reporter? With his head in his hands, the editor of Radio Wales News pondered how they were going to deal with things. In a recent phone-in there'd been a strong wave of protest against intruding in the man's private life, and he was finding it hard to explain how any coverage of the sex-change was going to be in the public interest. The editor regaled his colleagues with a tale about the war years when the BBC sent out truth to fight the Nazi propaganda machine. One night a stentorian newsreader announced to the People of Free Europe, 'Good evening, this is the British Broadcorping Castration.' How appropriate.

Around him there was a scrum of competing voices. Ian Bridei, the head of the Political Unit was making reference to a poll which suggested that were Keiron to stand for election in his native Newtown he would win with 98% support.

'There's something Messianic about it, there really

is. He's more than just a rugby player; he's the fullest expression of people's desires and the oath finder to how to realise them. Even soccer fans love him. Even people who hate rugby and all other sports love him. He's the most quotable sports player in the history of any game, and even though what he's doing flies in the face of the most fundamental machismo at the heart of rugby all the men love him and all the women love him. Should the Iranians launch a missile strike against Israel it would have to take second place on our news agenda to Keiron's tackle, as it were.'

They decided to do a live outside broadcast from the car park of the clinic and started making calls to get permission to park the satellite truck. Keiron's op was happening on the same day as a Welsh game. It had a certain elegance.

Marrying a steady hand with an accomplished eye, the glinting blade of the scalpel cuts through the flesh, the tiny pipette vacuuming away the blood. The surgeon cuts against the grain of the flesh, as if preparing carpaccio from Keiron's muscular brisket. High class removals, that's what the anesthetist calls it.

Without their star player, their dependable totem, Wales only scraped a win against an Italian side that had all the power of a Panzer division in their forward line. At half time the LCD display pumped out the message 'Get Well Soon'.

Outside the clinic, the chief reporter studies the unfamiliar lexicon she is going to use for the first of her live broadcasts. There are the unchangeable facts such as the Adam's apple, the one thing Keiron can't change other than shrink it in size, and then there all the other options such as 'suction-assisted lipoplasty of the waist, rhinoplasty, facial bone reduction, the conventional face-lift, and blephroplasty'. As stories go this one was supremely different, she had to give him that. She mouthed the words again. Ble-phro-plasty. On in five.

Six hours later and the effects of the gas had worn off. Keiron, in his private room, reached between his legs. He was as smooth as a Gilbey's match play rugby ball. There were three weeks to go before the next international and he was determined to play, against medical advice, without insurance if it came to that.

Wales' next game was a clash of juggernauts: Croker Park in Dublin. On that fateful Saturday the Irish were taking no prisoners and were going to take Keiron out. They were sick to the gills of hearing about him on TV and radio. They knew he'd been advised by all the medical staff not to play so soon after the operation but he'd said, with a cocky arrogance, that he'd take just one precaution, namely that he wasn't going to be tackled by anyone. Which was a big ask of anyone, especially as he was a marked man. Man? Huh! The Irish coach had found himself in a vat of hot water when he suggested that Wales was starting with just fourteen men. Keiron was impervious to such bear baiting. In the changing room before the game Keiron asked if anyone had any objections to his putting a hundred points on them.

'I'll need all your help mind. I'm still a bit delicate after the operation so if you could just block a few tackles when they're coming my way that would be just hunky dory.' His team members surrounded him as a phalanx and said they'd defend him to the death.

It was a capacity crowd and they were expecting such a gargantuan TV audience that the engineers in the control room of the National Grid were predicting a huge energy drain at half time as kettles went on across the land. An economist on Radio Wales predicted that the equivalent to eleven million pints of beer would be drunk in pubs, clubs and homes across the land. He also surmised a slump in economic productivity on Monday should Wales win and a worse slump if they lost.

The Royal Welsh Fusiliers band couldn't be heard above the hubbub. All of the television commentary focused on Keiron and for the BBC coverage they'd taken the unusual step of ascribing two cameras just to him, so they could follow his every move. The crowd had made placards to show their support. 'She's the Best', said one. 'Never Miss a Try', said another.

When the teams took to the pitch there was an unearthly roar.

When Keiron came out, already a little curvy from the hormones, the Welsh fans drummed up ecstasies. During the warm-up many in the crowd scrutinised the images of him on the big screen, curious to see the physical changes and, most importantly, because of a nervousness that 'losing your tackle means losing your tackle' as one newspaper pundit put it.

The Irish side had marked him for as many bone crunchers as they could mete out. It wasn't just his fiery skills they wanted to dampen down but also the buzz of idolatry that was generated around him. If they could break him they could break the team. It was a brave move and an unpopular one. But first they had to catch him. From the opening whistle, when Ireland's kick off ball landed squarely in the cradling arms of one of the Welsh props there was a confidence about the Welsh team that verged on a swagger. They ran forward with fluency and took risks as if these were the closing moments of the match, not the opening salvos of what settled into a fully fledged physical game at the first set piece. The Irish scrum seemed like an advert for steroids, their legs pedaling like cyclists and the front row pushing forward in an outrageous muscle surge. The Welsh pack wasn't just taken aback but were taken back, losing fifteen yards because of this almighty push.

The ball sped out and would have passed deftly all along the back line until Keiron managed to intercept a pass and started a slightly loping run with the crowd baying him on. He had caught the Irish napping. To the delight of the Welsh fans Keiron had enough time to do a little twirl and allow his behind to offer a hint of a waggle before putting Wales' first points on the board. And then, in an expression of excitement lifted from the manual of football hysteria, the Welsh players queued up to kiss him and both the irony and unity of the gesture wasn't lost on the crowd. Fifteen men. Fifteen men.

By half way through Wales were a scarlet flow of jerseys queuing up to penetrate the Irish defensive line, which held solid until Keiron chipped a ball over their heads, to be picked up with the dexterity of a basketball star by his best friend Martin. He landed on the touchline and threw Keiron a theatrical kiss, which was the moment above all others that showed how totally the team accepted him. They couldn't treat him as a woman yet, but they could show their team mate a good time, even as they took on the reigning world champs. It was like a first date.

The Irish came within a centimetre of replying with a try but had it disallowed by the fourth official. This might have been the thing that stoked up the spleen, this might have been what caused the Irish wing, Andy Shankleton, to stop a charging run by Keiron by bringing his knee up into his groin, which not only crumpled him but caused a rivulet of red to run down one thigh. The crowd was in uproar and the doctors couldn't sprint on fast enough for them, especially as the BBC had by now mixed both of the dedicated cameras, which intrusively showed a man in agony on a stretcher dripping blood. Such was the fury of the crowd that when Shankelton was peremptorily sent off one of the crowd threw a thermos flask at him, which hit him on the head and nobody was that shocked.

On television half time had precious little analysis of the game itself. Everyone wanted to know how Keiron was and the pitch-side commentator went to stand outside the medical room. A minute before the second half resumed the Welsh team came out of the tunnel with Keiron leading in front, where the captain should have been. The play-side reporter tossed a question at him, asking him how he was and he quipped, 'Guess I won't be having children now, Sharon,' which was relayed to a delightedly relieved crowd in the stadium and to millions of viewers who took a huge collective sigh of relief. It was also revealed that Hemmings the captain had voluntarily given Keiron the captain's shirt as he thought that would rack up the pressure on the green shirts even further.

Down to fourteen men the Ireland team struggled to keep the ball and deal with the fact that they were booed at every turn. The gap between them opened to over fifty points and the crowd wanted to pile on the humiliation which was now being doled out because of the heinous act against Keiron. Keiron who, three minutes before the final whistle, ran almost the whole length of the pitch and made a point of making sure that every Irish player was in the tally of those who wanted to catch him, but he ran rings around them all. He ran with joy and humour and when he finally touched the ball down as if it were an egg, and took a careful curtsey just before an Irish player came in late towards him, it was the best moment in the whole history of rugby union. Everyone agreed, apart from the sullen Irish.

That night, when an Aral sea's worth of ale was downed in the city, surgeons were working to contain Keiron's blood-loss. There had been a news blackout on how serious things were. By three in the morning, they had managed to staunch the flow but not enough to stop Keiron announcing his retirement from his bedside to a friendly reporter who needed the money such an exclusive could generate.

'I want to quit while I'm ahead,' said Keiron before he fell back into an opiate determined dream, in which he danced a funny sexy jig in a gold lamé dress on a big glass stage, and the crowd of seventy eight thousand rugby fans roared at him as he started his slinky, sensual dance to the accompaniment of a Donna Summer clubmix, which blasted out of the stadium P.A., a resounding celebration of his proper gender.

Picture Perfect

Each day, as the bills came tumbling through the letter box, Louis Morris wondered whether he could keep the wolf from the door. Or rather the slavering, mad-eyed, yellow-toothed pack of wolves from the door: his creditors. He was not exactly managing his finances well. The gas threatened cut-off. The electricity gave him ten days to devise a repayment plan. The sofa company had taken the sofa and the matching pouffe and the men who took it seemed gleeful in their work. Being a conceptual artist in south Wales in the new millennium was a vicious kind of pauperism.

He was also overdrawn on inspiration. If inspiration is like seeing a film you haven't seen, he was nowhere near a cinema. If it's like a story that falls from the sky, the sky above was bankrupt. No phosphorus moments, no Damascene insight.

At the start of May he'd got an Arts Council grant and started a series of what he called Soft Architectures. The money had helped him pay off one of his credit cards. In the foyer of the Taliesin arts centre in Swansea, Louis had made a series of skyscrapers using tufts of moss which he'd moulded in a press to make little green bricks, challenging the old saw that you can't ever make a multi-storey building out of sphagnum.

As part of a short tour of his work he exhibited his soft architecture in a park in Aberdare and at the National Botanic Gardens at Middleton Hall. A critic from the *Observer* travelled down to see them and wrote a positive and lyrical piece under the heading 'Frozen Music'. A German, probably Goethe, once described architecture as frozen music to which the *Observer* guy had replied by suggesting that, therefore, music might be defrosted architecture. Louis also had a three page spread in the *Telegraph* magazine and a four minute piece filmed about him on 'The Culture Show'.

His cash flow was less of a sluggish stream in June as he'd been commissioned to arrange a civic pyrotechnics show for Fife Council. After a gruelling bus journey to Scotland, he met the alderman of the council, a boozy-looking man who had jowls like a very ancient orang-utan, who said 'they don't want art, son, so concentrate on big bangs. They like flash and bang, flash and bang. Clear?'

Morris had made an extraordinary series of fireworks where the fuse wasn't a flame hissing trail of nitrate cord but rather a blend of powdered aluminium and iodine. The components of this cocktail remained inert until water was added as a catalyst and the whole shebang went kapow! In the construction of his ingenious fuse, water was added, drip by drip, from a strategically positioned pipette. He imagined the alderman's face turning puce with delight: two kilos of aluminium dust and the same amount of iodine, all packed tightly into a container. Kaboom! There were purple clouds over the East Fife hills that night, a toxic sunset painted by Turner.

Louis Morris was anything if not a hard worker. He was no scrounger on the state: he worked for the good of his soul and seldom asked for grants. It was just that Louis was at the mercy of the art-economy in a poor country. To compound the problem he gave a hell of a lot of work away for free. It didn't happen to plumbers, or radiographers. They weren't asked to do stuff for fuck all.

In his last year at art school, being taught by razzled old soaks who still thought the future belonged to the Vorticists, he knew that there was no other furrow to follow. He did various jobs to pay his student way and later on to shore up his ambitions. He did zombie shifts as a night watchman. One night his eyelids grew heavy and he completely missed a lorry pulling into the yard, hitching up to a trailer full of deep freezes before skedaddling. He was given the sack, but not before a Hollywood grilling by a CID man with bad breath like peat bog methane and an attitude that rolled good-cop, bad-cop all into one.

Louis desperately needed a new idea, something like Damien Hirst's diamond skull. He strolled down to the art school library and ambled through their holdings of books and video. He liked Robert Wilson's high definition television portraits of Hollywood stars and Bill Viola's video work. He leafed through Sam

Taylor-Wood's book of portraits in which she restaged famous paintings. Then it came to him: a moment when the mind's pinball machine lights up like a miniature Vegas.

Ten minutes later he made a call to the Commissioning Editor for Wales Channel One programmes and booked himself an appointment for the following Monday. Louis bought a bottle of Beringer 1997 Cabernet Sauvignon to celebrate and sat on his stool – his only remaining stick of furniture – to sip it appreciatively.

Monday morning came and his heart was beating out a rumba of excitement. The woman who came to meet him in Channel One's reception was a total glamour puss, perched precariously on the highest heels and radiating that superior confidence that comes from being a P.A. to power. Madeleine ushered him into a wood-panelled room with a couple of leather sofas that spoke of Sicilian vespers and Renaissance light. There was a large desk as a centre-piece and a cupboard full of awards. Rose de Montreux. Royal Television Society. BAFTAS. Investors in People.

'Do sit down. Can I offer you a drink of some kind? Mr Fopp won't be very long. He's just with a Chinese investor.'

Louis said he was fine and waited. When Arnie Fopp walked into the room he did so with a swagger. Louis knew that here was a no-nonsense type.

'A pleasure to meet you. I feel as if I've known you a long time already. I have some of your works, you know. Three in fact, including "Narrow Man".'

'Narrow Man' was one of Louis' own favourites – a

charcoal, figurative work where the eponymous subject seemed crammed in between the edges of the paper. He had huge hands like trenching tools. Louis still thought it might be the nearest he'd got to capturing the human condition. It was also the one he'd been most sorry to part company with. Mr Fopp had taste.

'So what's the idea you've brought me?'

And so Louis settled into the luxurious embrace of the sofa and pitched his pitch.

'You know there have been some big series about Welsh art in the past decade or so. Painting the Dragon and then the one where they created a virtual gallery and plonked it down in St Justinians on the Pembrokeshire coat. Well I have an idea where we bring the paintings to life…'

'What, like an animation series?'

'No, they'd be short dramas. We'd show how things were five minutes before the moment of a painting was captured and five minutes afterwards. We find out what the characters were thinking. Bring the story alive. Bring the dead people in the painting alive.'

Fopp got it straight away. He proved it by getting his secretary to invite a man from finance and a man from contracts to meet them on the office verandah which looked out over the retail park. The carve-up of the BBC licence fee was in everybody's sights. You didn't need to be a greedy porker to want a slice of that cake.

Over drinks and a half hour of the most delicious salacious gossip about local TV stars, Fopp said he wanted to offer Louis a chance to make a pilot. Not any old pilot, but one where there was more than adequate resourcing. He'd need a big drama-style budget, suggested Fopp, looking at the finance director who looked ill at ease, probably working out the cost of the rare olorosos being sipped.

'Start on it soon, and we'll be able to squeeze it under the wire of this financial year.'

He mentioned a figure and it was as much as Louis could do not to choke on his sherry. This was a better result than Louis could have wished for. The last time he'd pitched a TV idea it was in a meeting with the undead, three cadavers in a room who only moved to say goodbye: leave your name in the wastepaper basket on the way out.

Louis borrowed a mobile phone from his mate Keith so he could make the calls he needed to. Louis was in Companies House that afternoon, setting up a limited company which he called 'Canvassing'. The finance director said he'd be able to front the development money within a week, so he'd need bank details by the weekend. Later that afternoon, in a daze of happiness, Louis met his bank manager, a beleaguered soul who always laughed at the extravagant inventiveness of his excuses: some burglars stole the cooker so I'll need a new one was a favourite. Louis left the bank with a company account. When he got home he designed a logo on the Mac he'd borrowed from his long-suffering brother, printed off some letter headings and he was in business.

The weekend meandered past just as surely as the rivulet of red wine ran down his throat, acquired from the office where the owner who gave him a VAT receipt for two cases of the stuff marked 'office equipment'. On the Monday he had a meeting with a guy called Larry, who'd made two or three films. Louis liked his style, but most of all he'd been wowed by his gift for composition.

'I'd like you to work on a project of mine. We're going to bring paintings to life. We're going to start local, with some of my own Welsh faves, and if the idea takes off, I don't know, we could end up bringing the Last Supper to life with De Niro as Jesus.'

'I like your overvaulting ambition,' replied Larry, who wasn't his usual ebullient self. He was still smarting from a review of his latest mini-soap opera in the *Sunday Telegraph* in which A. A. Gill had said that it has as much drama as painting of a fruit bowl. The same fucker had said that his drama series the previous year had the plot of a gibbon colony. Gill was typical of the reaction from the rest of the snakes. So Larry didn't just need to work on a new project, he needed something that would allow him to walk tall again. Louis's project sounded as if it might have that power. It even sounded as if it was that rarity: a new idea for television, the stuff that drew awards like a magnet.

'When do you plan to start?' asked Larry.

'Dispatch is my middle name. We start next week?'

'We'll need a writer P.D.Q. Someone I can sit in a room with for a day or two and then be back with a script that works like a Swiss watch. A tall order I know.'

'I know the very man. If he's on the wagon he can deliver. And if he's canned when I ring, we'll need to wait a day for him to get his shit together. Have you met Trefor Gruffydd? Old school in every way. Working on just one kidney but a man with a gift. He wrote the last Bond movie.'

When he arrived the next day the screenwriter looked like the very epitome of an old soak. His face was a map of burst blood vessels.

'Larry tells me you're going to resuscitate dead painters, blow life back into them.' The man smelled of cooking oil. He had more hair coming out of his ears than anyone Louis had ever seen before.

'Something like that. Take a look at this...' he handed Gruffydd a book called *The Visual Culture of Wales* and there was a photograph of the painting Louis wanted to start with.

'It's called "The Communist". What we have to do is work out what brought all these people together and then figure out what happened next.'

'It's a strong image, no doubt about that. It's a sort of crucifixion. The main figure is a sacrifice?'

'That's how I've always seen it.'

That day they made their way through eight cafetières of coffee, a dozen bagels with cream cheese and smoked salmon and a large bowl of fruit. The surges of blood sugar made their brains race.

'He's about to soar up to heaven to meet his maker. Or his father. Or what if this was an early experiment with helium? The gas is a by-product of whatever's made in this manufactory and the man in the red waistcoat...'

'Let's call him Thomas John.'

'So Thomas John has just taken in a huge amount of helium or even a newly discovered gas that simply lifts you off the ground: "The Human Zeppelin" flies for the first time.'

'A legendary circus act.'

'And his claim to fame is that he can float over the crowds without the use of hidden wires as his great rival Mephisto employs.'

'So instead of staging his act in a marquee like all the others – the hundreds of inferior performers who can only dream of achieving what he has – he allows the crowd to choose where exactly he's going to perform. And this time it's a factory. Somewhere in the Swansea valley, where they've parted with a sum of money far in excess of a guinea between them for the privilege of seeing him levitate above their heads. But this time he floats out the window and drifts away on the wind, so that the last thing they see is the merest speck of him heading over the Beacons towards the east.'

A brief pause, a mouthful of bagel.

'What if he's the victim of some awful accident and that's the way he's now forced to stand?'

'Being used as an example of the callousness of the factory owners when it comes to anyone who wants to kick-start a strike.'

They had a good day, throwing up a legion of ideas, but at the end they had to settle for the obvious. Gruffydd went off to write it, a waver in his walk as if his body always remembered being drunk.

The Locations Manager, Elen, scouted around the riven gulches of the south Wales valley looking for a suitable building with a view of smoke stacks. She searched the whole length of the Rhymney valley right up to where it merged into swathes of white moor grass. And found the perfect place.

The shoot was scheduled to start on a Monday. Gruffydd delivered the script a week before and the actor, who'd been chosen to play the Communist, Peter Fry, was dressed by the best costume lady in the land. The Stardust Agency supplied twenty extras, who chomped their way through an entire van load of bacon butties before they started filming.

Louis called 'Action!' and the great creature Illusion was awakened in his lair. That's how he saw it, fancifully, and he was the boss.

The men had been told that the owners, the Crabtrees, were going to shut the strikers outside the factory and if needs be bring in scabs to work their shifts. A sulphur-coloured sun lit up the bracken-covered hills, which themselves seemed tinged with brimstone as the determined men marched towards the churchyard at Moriah in Penydarren, where they were due to gather to work out their tactics. They had already been told of how the soldiers had broken the strike at Abermardy after three consecutive nights of defenestration and an appalling incident where a police horse had been blinded and another killed with a brick.

The sound of hobnails marching in determined unison resounded around the terraces. You could smell determination in the air. The world was marching. This part of the world was a soup, a cawl of people from all over. Staten Island would be hard pressed to match the relentless magnetism that drew in men from Cardiganshire, from Somerset, Cornwall and Lancashire too. Women marched with the men and one of them, from the Somerset levels, stood up to address the gathering in an accent thick as churned butter. They worked just as hard as the men, she argued, as did the children who worked for a pittance.

The foment of revolution had begun in the public houses and early libraries. The workers had read incendiary books and explosive pamphlets. They had absorbed broadsides which railed against the world order; conduits in bright bindings for new ideas concocted in European cafés and argued for with all the vehemence of Old Testament prophets.

The crowd had swollen now and they filled the square next to the church. A man railed against injustice and castigated the newspapers, which weren't to be trusted since the proprietors drank in the same clubs as the mine owners and foundry owners. The crowd bustled him along with the ease of moving a baby in swaddling. He kept on talking in his preacherly way all the while.

The man was called Morgan Davies and had given them a heady sermon, offering his unvarnished view to the crowd, which was mesmerised by the smoldering passion of his voice and the felicity of the examples he had chosen. He told them how heedless some men can be about the lives of others.

'About the same time that Peter the Great was using huge numbers of men to haul granite into a swamp to create his great city, there were so many serfs working the land that in one of the great estates there was a serf orchestra. Because there were so many serfs the estate owners didn't bother to teach them to read music but just told them when to play the one note they knew. And when one of them died from exhaustion there was always another to take his place. This meant that life was worthless; the value of a man less than a horse, much, much less than a horse.'

A cloth-capped crowd ringed him in now.

'Behold the man,' he continued, 'behold the man who stands before you and says that all this must change.'

His arms were stretched out, as if invisibly nailed into the rank air, his back rigid with self-belief.

'Behold the man who says that I, a communist, believe that our struggle is universal, and that the principles we uphold are pit props to shore up the dignity of man. We will allow the working man to hold his head up high. We will restore his dignity.'

And as if the word 'high' was a cue for some ingenious magic trick, where all the mechanical contraptions were hidden by slight of hand, Morgan's hob-nailed boots left the ground, the bulk of his belly weightless now. Within half a minute Morgan Davies started to levitate above the ground; first, some six feet in the air and then, as if he weighed no more than a small ball of chaffinch-feather-down, it seemed as if his body was caught by a breeze and he was lifted higher as he was still orating. But soon the words became dislocated: 'shackles', 'a lack of poverty' and, finally, when he was two hundred yards or so in the air, just the single word 'Megan', the name of his wife, drifted down to them as they all watched open-mouthed as his body floated high above the smoke stacks and drifted east. The crowd was silent now, witnesses to an event that some would attack as being the devil's work and historians would see as the extraordinary seed of the strike that followed.

'Cut,' said the first assistant director as the camera crane reached its full height and the thin wires from the other crane became taut after slinging the stunt man skywards.

Louis and Larry had been transfixed by the sequence as they viewed it on the monitor. A childhood verse, learned in Sunday school, had flashed across Louis' brain. Something about the meek, he thought, struggling to remember the religious cliché. The phrase escaped him.

'It's a wrap,' said Louis. 'Clear the set. See you tomorrow, bright and early. We're doing Renoir, so all you smokers get some Gitanes and we can save a small fortune on dry ice.'

The stunt man was lowered down, but he was changed somehow. There were twin candles of wisdom burning in his eyes. He went home a changed man, so much so that his wife accused him of seeing someone else. And in a way he had, hanging there in his harness, looking up at endless space.

Taste Bud Alert

High overhead, a swarth-backed gull flew to its island roost. By now too late in the day to fish, it ignored a turmoil of mackerel in the sound beneath, its metronome wings purposeful as it flew towards an Apache sun. It was a one-off sunset, a backdrop for lovers' trysts. The gull diminished in the hushed air as the horizon magnetised the silver Christmas-bauble which hung on invisible threads.

In the prison ship, the S.S. Madagascar, the summoning bell for dinner was greeted by the groans of close on three hundred wannabe Epicureans, who knew that once again they were going to be badly let down. Tony Redbone, the cook who warmed the slop, didn't bother with taste, concentrating on volume instead. His face was a little off-putting as he had what could be mistaken for hygiene issues, with a vivid skin condition that verged on the tropical, something wrong with his blood that made it a veritable harvest of pustules, which made his skin resemble subcutaneous minestrone soup.

Tonight's desperate menu was themed around

potatoes: a cheese and potato part-bake with added mashed potatoes on top. It wasn't meant to be part-baked, but that's the way it turns out if you forget to ratchet up the ovens, so that the potatoes were crunchy and cold. To make matters worse, the inmates weren't allowed salt cellars after the incident when a nonce called Pippy Evans had a cellar implanted by a pair of Old Time gangsters called Scissors Eddie and Morris the Gimp. So salt had joined the list of prison barter items, along with aftershave, smack, wacky baccy, pornographic comics and various pills. And the phrase 'Pass the salt, Morris' entered the fearful ledger of prison legends, invoking images of Pippy the child molester, his eyes wide open with fear.

The prisoners hated Tony Redbone for never investigating the pages of a cook-book. They dreamed of crème brûlées, Thai green chicken curries and Caesar salad, all just out of reach, like Tantalus' bunch of grapes. In a vision, serried ranks of waiters appeared to one inmate, bearing an array of silver salvers from which he had to choose one. He chose badly, choosing potato part-bake. Luck of the draw. Other prisoners simply had nightmares about spending fifteen years eating their way through nothing other than Tony's bill of fare. They'd been to other nicks, and this was by far the worst. By far the most indigestible. The food at Dartmoor was Michelin standard by comparison. A common dream involved a conveyor belt along which passed an array of foodstuffs. Macaroni cheese. Fresh apple tart. Roast lamb with mint sauce. Jesus!

They complained to Mr Snee the governor, who

wrote down the names of the complainants and said he'd see to it that the menus would be changed. The ravenous prisoners set their taste buds on yellow alert in preparation for an expected cavalcade of flavours, but nothing happened. As the governor reasoned, this was prison after all, not the Dorchester. The men weren't here for their health.

A plot born of resentment and grumbling stomachs was hatched on the Madagascar. One night the Morse code tapped out along the pipes dispersed a message to all three decks and even into solitary, where Jimmy Bucket was learning to regret leaving a roach in the ashtray after what had turned out to be a rather stunning skunkweed joint. When the screws found the roach they gave him twenty one days in the brig, straight off. Jimmy was a bit slow at deciphering Morse – perhaps a delirious effect of all the dope – and when he spelled out the message in his head he had to go over it a couple of times to make sure he had got the gist of it.

The men on every level of the ship considered the import of the messages. The tapping punctuated the night. Donations were invited: to hire a man, or to kidnap the cook's wife. All they wanted Tony to do was learn to cook, read Mrs Beeton or something. Jimmy liked their thinking. Along with pretty much everyone else onboard he'd throw in a couple of sovs. He had five years left of the appalling food regime. It was breaking his spirit far more than his time in the airless black chamber.

They got fifteen grand together in a night, mainly in the form of promissory notes, although some of the more powerful lags contributed actual fifty pound notes. Natcho kept the tally while Morris the Gimp, who had just got back after a couple of transfers – Wakefield, where they served curries on a Friday, and Albany, where they had a bleedin' nutritionist for fark's sake – took care of the practical arrangements, putting the job out to tender, sealed bids, the usual form.

They had three applications but they had to discount one right away because everyone knew that David Hangood had died in a car crash and that his wife was trying to carry on the family business using his name, but everybody knew that she was a crap assassin, what with her short-sightedness and asthma and all. She was game, though, you had to give it to her. And skint, so they sent her a little something just for having a bash. The other two bids came from class acts – both anonymous but with impressive CVs. The inmates made their decision. They gave their instructions and let the act unfold.

When Tony got the summons to come up to the governor's quarters, his mind instantly fled to his recent scam. He'd found a new source of meat for Thursdays from a Romany turf accountant who worked down the dog track. His heart rate rose as he ran through the possible ways he'd have been rumbled. When he stepped through the white, steel-plate door the gravity of the man's demeanour suggested something worse, much worse.

'Sit down Tony. I'm afraid I have some bad news as we find ourselves in a very delicate situation…'

'I can explain everything,' blurted Tony, but there was something so serious about the governor's eyes that he desisted there and then.

'Your wife has been kidnapped and whoever's taken her hostage is demanding better food on board.'

Without a moment's hesitation Tony volunteered his resignation, but while the governor said his alacrity was commendable he suggested that Tony should watch the video from the kidnappers first.

The images were high definition, captured by a camera hand that was steady and sure. His wife, Florrie, seemed unfazed by the situation and Tony remembered the first time he had realised that he was in love with her. They were walking along the pebble shore in Brighton on a blustery day that seemed to throw seagulls around like confetti. She was wearing a fisherman's yellow coat and a sou'wester and looked as if she usually worked way out in the North Sea. He was suggesting she was overdressed when a violent squall, coupled with a freak wave, threw an enormous cascade of water over them and he remembered them spluttering their laughter as she raised her hands to show how dry she was and he tried to shake water out of his drenched woollen coat like a terrier coming out of a drain.

This was the image on the television screen – a brave, resourceful woman who enunciated very clearly what the kidnappers wanted and that she would be released only after the governor made an announcement during dinner hour that things would improve. She made it sound as if she was reading out a letter to him.

'They say it's nothing personal and they don't want you to lose your job. But they do want you to learn to cook. And you can understand where they're coming from can't you, Tone? Anyway, they're looking after me very well and there's one of them who's got a sense of humour just like yours. Do what you can to get me released soon.'

The Governor looked at Tony and Tony looked back.

'My problem is twofold. I can't be seen to be letting in to the demands of the kidnappers and I need to keep my authority whatever happens.'

Tony, who had a lot of 'O' levels, even though catering skills wasn't one of them, had two suggestions. In a conspiratorial tone he asked if anyone else knew about the tape, suggesting that this was a secret the inmates could collectively keep. He then had his brainwave. Why didn't they get Jamie Oliver, the celebrity chef involved?

That night Tony smoked his way through a carton of fags and the governor stared at the bulb on the ceiling as he thought things through: how authority could be sanctioned by the prisoners as well as the guards and how Tony's crazy scheme was worth a punt. The governor liked life on board ship, it was the nearest he'd ever get to being a naval captain and ever since he was a nipper, growing up in a terraced house in Rochdale, he'd harboured a dream of gold braid and white uniform and a litany of sea names and far off gulfs: Cortez, Mediterranean, Bering, Baltic, Mexico, South China. He tried to imagine how he would live with himself if he conspired with a ship full of Category A prisoners to keep a secret. He was convinced that they could keep a secret because of the watchwords 'what happens inside stays inside'. There were hard men, with hard histories, who took wives in jail but no-one would ever know. There were brotherhoods that didn't follow divisions of race or creed, but of desire. The Governor only understood the half of it but he knew that if he made a pact it would be not with one devil but with two hundred and fifty eight of them.

The civil servant who took the call thought at first that he had a loco caller who'd somehow minnowed through the net, because all he heard was the word 'Madagascar' and Terence Minns could only think of lemurs. But when the Governor of the prison ship Madagascar started to explain his plan, Terry knew enough to ring his mate Phil who was a political special adviser and knew exactly how to make political capital out of pretty much anything. This governor, he explained, had phoned him up with an idea about asking Jamie Oliver to visit the ship to start a campaign to improve prison food. He'd cited a study in Texas that suggested prisoners who were given good food became better prisoners overall with even prisons such as the notorious Angola jail in Louisiana benefitting from regular gumbo and decent veg. Phil said he thought he was definitely onto something, what with the latest cock-up in the Middle East where British peacekeepers had bopped off a Hamas leader needing some good news story to knock it off the news agenda and so Phil phoned another New Labour apparatchik higher up the chain and by noon he was through to Number Ten who were taking the Madagascar proposal very seriously indeed.

Jamie Oliver's agent put down the phone with a look of extraordinary triumph. He'd never talked turkey with a politician before but he'd just talked to the Prime Minister's Private Secretary who'd agreed with him when he suggested that Jamie'd probably need a bit of a boost in his campaign to improve school dinners before moving on to prisons.

The press conference was one of the best attended in the recent history of the Prison Service and the news that Jamie Oliver had assembled a team of notorious murderers, robbers, rapists and one satanist who had boiled his own child in a chip pan had filled two helicopter shuttles to the island, not to mention the TV technicians who had been ferrying back and forth with satellite stuff for three days or so.

It had been a major headache for the security services, especially with Al-Qaeda's fondness for marine targets such as the U.S. ship they had ramrodded off the coast, and the fact that all of the people they were dealing with were dangerous as vipers, not even mentioning that Oliver had said he wasn't interested in teaching people how to cook with plastic instruments, so these guys would be appearing live on TV armed with cleavers, knives, weapons' grade soup ladles and ferocious whisks.

Five. Four. Three. Two. One.

The whole thing was staged-managed for the Six O'Clock News in Britain, even though there were TV broadcasts going out in every time zone. There was something about this story that appealed to even the most life weary night editor and time served sub.

Cue governor Snee, who welcomed everyone and gave a potted history of the ship, which was mainly voiced-over by the newsreaders on their particular shows. Then it was the Prime Minister's turn because a top level strategy group had decided that the chef should have the lion's share of limelight. He kept his speech tersely short. Then Jamie was up.

'Thank you, Mr Prime Minister for your kind words and for the great support you have given to my campaign, no, let's call it this country's great campaign to convert our children from a generation that thinks food begins and ends with a burger to a huge group of bright kids who know when peas are in season and who rejoice in that time. But today we turn our attention to the incarcerated: criminals who have transgressed against society and are thus banished from society, but that doesn't mean that society should then forget about them once they're behind bars. That is a barbarian thought, the attitude of the sort of society that neglects its children and therefore itself. But today we begin a journey to improve the lives of those in prison, by giving them not just nutritious but delicious food.'

And with that Jamie strode into the brand new kitchen that had been installed on the lower deck. They helped him make an enormous paella. This extended news programme commanded a huge audience. Even the Prime Minister's personal ratings moved up a couple of notches.

A fortnight later Tony met his new assistant, who brought seven crates of provisions on board with him. He watched amazed at the briskness with which the man threw bits of chicken, duck and pork, noodles and ginger along with splashes of wine into one of the big pots.

'Fine banquet stock,' said the man, winking cheerily. 'Always start with the basics...' and then he explained about the fifty-six cooking methods they used, from chao through ruan zha to dong, which was all about jellying and freezing. Tony listened to him as if he was explaining how to build a space rocket.

Word had spread around the cells so that there was an excited chatter filling the place. The prisoners sounded like starlings. When they saw the screws laying out place settings for themselves as well as the prisoners, they knew something was up. When they saw chopsticks instead of knives they cheered within. Stylish, totally stylish. The men sat down as if in church. Even the governor graced them with his presence. And then they ate their fill. Tony had been reading Fiona Dunlop's book. Glory be! He had been reading a cookery book!

A great vat of jade web soup with quail eggs and bamboo pith fungus kicked things off, the fungus redolent of the bamboo forests, where 'fuming cataracts spill over rocky hillsides, over red earth and rocks', that date from when the world was young. They ate rabbit with rock sugar and succulent stewed meats, tea-smoked duck and coral-like snow lotus, a plant where the roots lie in mud but the blossom reaches to the sky as a symbol of Buddhist enlightenment. There were intriguing dishes such as ants climbing trees, where tiny morsels of meat clung like insects to the chopsticks. Bitter melons followed radish slivers, flavoured with dark tangerine peel. After the famine years their bowls overflowed with Gong Bao chicken with peanuts and a dish called Pockmarked Mother

Chen's bean curd, 'named after the smallpox-scarred wife of a Qing Dynasty restaurateur'. When the chef announced the name of this next dish through the serving hatch an old wag said 'Anything's better than pock-marked Tony's pasta' and even Tony himself laughed in a break from so much chopping. He had no idea cooking could be so labour intensive, how so few things came out of a tin.

The men washed everything down with a rivulet of green tea and there was something heartening about the way in which some of the younger men showed the older convicts how to use the chopsticks. Rounding off with silver ear fungus in crystal sugar soup and eight treasure rice pudding there wasn't a man among them – even the power lifters who burned through twelve thousand calories in a single session – who didn't feel replete, as full as a tick. They took away the photocopied menus which would take the place of bare-breasted women in the cells.

The governor stood up and asked the men to show their appreciation to Larry, the new assistant chef, and to Tony who'd slaved so hard to make this wonderful meal work. The men hooted and hollered, cheered fit to burst. There was a cascade of chopsticks, thrown in the air in appreciation.

Later on the Madagascar, a fug of flatulence settled like a sea mist throughout the levels. Prisoners patted their expanded stomachs. Boss hogs were sending leftovers to the nonces, yes, sending cold noodles to the child molesters, with bits of razor blade hidden in the mix. This was prison at the end of the day, and they were all at sea.

The Pit

Workers at Wales' last remaining deep pit, Tower Colliery near Hirwaun, had to abandon work yesterday when human remains were found in a recently excavated drift. Two bones, believed to be a femur and part of a collarbone, were taken away by police and are being examined at the Forensics Department in Bridgend.

Broadcast on BBC's Good Morning Wales, 6.9.07

The tunnels are long and preternaturally dark. Down there naked eyes are useless. In such recesses, where there isn't so much as a hint or a glint of light, the ears are forced to compensate, so the sound of a scurrying rat seems swollen to twice its size, the rustle of hairs on its rancid pelt like brushfire. This is the darkest labyrinth, the passageways connected in ways that no one remembers nowadays, now that the mine entrances are padlocked. After what happened down there.

There's a myth among miners that a robin sighted underground is a portent of death. A shot lighter was reported to have seen no fewer than four robins in a shaft at Caled Number Four.

Known by some as the 'deadliest colliery in Christendom', Caled Number Four, near the village of Maerdy was opened in 1873. It was one of the biggest employers in the industry as a whole. Three thousand and three men sweated and coughed there. Miners were like ants burrowing into Allt Y Fedwen following an incline called the Trimsaran Sink. The secondhand winding gear above ground was arthritic: when the big wheel turned it made the sound of a badger being flayed.

First timers, twelve or thirteen year olds on their virgin shift, would double-take when they saw the shot lighter who was blind and had to be shown where to place his fuses and how to light them. The man also had the shakes. But despite the creakingness of the machinery and the oddity of some of the senior men, Caled Number Four had rich seams of luscious coal, producing masses of hard nuggets that were long-burning and sought after by the Royal Navy for their Ironsides. But there was always something curious about the workings. Lit by candles, in defiance of marsh gas, surveyors who measured the growing tunnels could never quite make their sums add up. There always seemed to be more space than accounted for by their instruments. Roofways looked twenty feet bigger than the actual measurements. There were caverns that might have belonged to a forgotten race, halls of long lost kings, troglodyte rulers of the darkness under the land.

Davy Jones was a miner in Caled Number Four, though everyone called him Cross Eyes. When he was born they said that storm clouds had galloped down from the hills and lightning had struck the tree outside his mother's room. He was a lonely child because other children were merciless and the only friend he had was a girl who ran on sticks because of polio. She was called Catherine and kissed him once, full on the lips before apologising and saying she had the mumps. His parents were of that hard generation that never gave him love, so he grew up a stunted flower.

But he did get married, to a scrawny thing called Anne he met after chapel on the Monkey Walk: she loved him like life itself. They had a child though neither could work out exactly how that had come about. They rented a tiny terraced cottage above the canal with money he borrowed at a high rate of interest from his dad and bought two fine chairs so they could sit of an evening and discuss the previous Sunday's sermon. Davy might have said he was happy then. His wife's porcelain skin in the flickering light. The metronome ticking and tocking of his grandmother's grandfather clock. New potatoes from the garden where he'd planted autumn's peelings and seen them send up vernal shoots. But it was a brief happiness. The work at the mine dried up just before the General Strike and because he was proud and stubborn like his parents, Davy couldn't ask them for help when the money dwindled. He watched his wife turn skeletal and his baby run out of life. First the bawling stopped, then his whimpering, and finally Thomas stopped breathing. Anne faded like the last note on a pipe. So he had a bag of bones for a wife and a grey lump of flesh for a son.

His wife only lingered on this earth for some days.

Davy had to live with the image of the two tiny coffins in the graveyard at Gerazim, borne aloft so lightly on the shoulders of the bearers. It was an afternoon of sleeting rain. Davy's parents died soon after, leaving him alone to contemplate the savagery of his personal God. *Duw Cariad Yw* is what it said in the Bible. God is Love.

When the mine reopened after The Strike, some of the former workers were so rickety from lack of nutrition that their hips snapped as they crawled underground. One man's elbows broke when he reached up for a rope. Another snapped a vertebra just looking up. And among the legion of the starved, the most pitifully lean was Davy, with his pipe-cleaner legs and flesh so thin you'd swear you could see his heart beating if he left his shirt collar open wide enough. Some days, as he chipped forward with his hands bandaged to soak up the blood, he heard his son's crying as clearly as the church bell.

Davy might have worked out his days on earth in Number Four were it not for the tragic day when a runaway spake smithereened a dozen pit props as it careened its way down one of the deepest tunnels, breaking men's bodies like snapping chicken bones.

Hitting the bottom, the reverberations set off a rumbling reaction in the earth and almost all Caled's labyrinth of tunnels collapsed amid whirlwinds of cloying dust.

He might have been concussed for a day or more. When Davy opened his eyes he could see nothing in the pitch dark but was aware of a burning pain in his right shoulder where it had been severed from the arm by a falling mass of coal. The weight of it pressing down on him had staunched the flow of blood, had near cauterised it, while threatening to collapse his rib cage. The arm lay there in the dark, its fingers, despite the congealing of the blood, making attractive suckling for a rat, the only other living creature in the tunnels. He coughed, and Davy could hear nothing other than the tiny claws of the animal scarpering, his blood on its whiskers.

He had no sense of time other than the rate at which his hunger gnawed inside. It grew in intensity so that his mind was filled with images of cauldrons of his mam's cawl, with luscious aromas. He had visitations of marmalade, bore witness to hallucinations featuring sides of hanging bacon.

On the third day, Davy casually picked up the limb and sucked his own forearm, knowing that meat lasted long underground, something about the air, or the depth away from the sun, or the near absence of microbial life. Something, anyway. It was a white taste and without thinking about it he drove his incisors into the meat, and started tearing chunks away from the tendons. He carried on until he was sated and at that point the rush of nutrition gave him sufficient strength to attempt to lift the fractured spar of wood that had him pinned to the floor. It lifted, slowly at first, but then with a magical strength, he lifted it as if it were balsa. On his one hand and two knees he crawled along the floor, five fingers splayed out before him, searching in the dust for a candle, which he managed to light with the flint box he always carried with him.

It was a garden of broken limbs, white tulip hands

breaking through the dust stratum, faces of his friends now flattened or wrecked out of recognition, staring at him like dumb watermelons. He ate William Trefor's buttocks over a three-day period, savouring the vague hint of carbolic soap which adhered to his skin. Him being a miner, William's obsessive cleanliness had always provided a rich topic for conversation.

As he grew braver, Davy started on soft parts, spilled brain matter. The goodness hovered up from Matthew Dunvant's, along with a last supper of partly digested cheese and bread. Except for the sinewy footballers, he found some of the younger colliers quite succulent.

It was only on the fifteenth day that Davy managed to stand up straight in one of the chamber tunnels. By now his candles were long expired but he found two places where the tiniest glimmers of light filtered through along with rainwater which pooled dangerously now that the pumps were no longer working. His nails now felt strong as he started to scratch on a soft patch of coal and he found that soon he was making real progress, especially when he started to use his teeth as well, biting off gobbets of coal and spitting them out even as his nails made a high screeching sound.

He made it into the next colliery in the valley and decided to lie in wait, a lizard waiting for the fly. The father of three he snapped up was trailing his butties on the way back to the spake when Davy nabbed him, dispatching him with a spade. He dragged him into an air vent and started with the eyes, as if he were eating caramels.

And so he continued – always on the move –

snacking as he went, or if he got a fat one staying awhile so that he grew plumper – reserves of energy he drew on as he moved across the coalfield. From feast to famine he went, investigating closed workings and thriving mines, able to gnaw through the earth like a rat through a ship's hawser. On and on, forever hungry and seldom sated. Blaenyrhaca. Pergwm. Abercwmnedd. Tyle One and Tyle Two. Along Ogmore and Rhymney, shadowing the rivers in their courses and unlocking floods and terrors.

In 1963 there was a sighting. A hydrologist, checking out some pipe casings in the pit in Wyattstown heard a strange scuffling sound and then saw a deformed man run down a tunnel. By the time his description had been repeated around a frightened village the man had grown: his globular cross eyes were the size of sinner plates, like a gargantuan barn owl with a squint. The man's nails were those of a pantomime Mandarin and his deformed hump of a back thrashed around in the collective imagination like an eel stretching on dry land. The teeth, man, they were as big as stalactites! I heard he chased this man and ran so fast the man only got away by wriggling out of his coat! After that, teams armed with police truncheons were sent to check every part of the mine, but to no avail. The monster was made of Scotch mist. He seeped away like a breath of methane.

It was Prime Minister Margaret Thatcher who did for Davy. As she took on the unions and closed down the mines throughout the United Kingdom, so too did she eliminate Davy's source of food. But there were side benefits to the Thatcher era, too. The police had less money to spend on trying to catch the monster that the popular imagination had cast like a Grendel inhabiting the land of fear. The National Coal Board was forced to up the danger money for anyone who worked underground. Police investigators over the decades remained dumbfounded that they hadn't so much as a single decent clue to go on.

And then the last pit in Wales closed and Davy could no longer smell so much as a molecule of new prey, for all his desperate, snuffling peregrinations along drift and through hard surfaces. So he had to leave the subterranean world. He had to go to the Overground, where meat was plentiful. He managed to make his home there, found a way to live. Snaring and surviving, stalking unwitting prey, along the empty aisles of late night supermarkets.

Recently there was another sighting, behind the loading bay of Tesco in Llansamlet. But not enough of a sighting for the scared man to tell his mates, as he'd been drinking on shift.

He's seen a man seemingly bent over on himself, dragging something heavy in the direction of the overspill car park.

Davy'd nabbed a man behind household goods, stunned him with a brick, the swiftly pulled him through some plastic flaps into the stockroom and through the back doors where some men were unloading pallets. Pulling the carcass swiftly now, as if it were on a sled, he got it out onto the ramp and pulled it with a dull thump to the ground, his actions urged on by hunger.

Safe in a clump of rhododendron, Davy scrutinised

his victim: plenty there for a long feast. The miner got out a knife, a fork and a threadwire saw, ideal for cutting bone. He started carving, pulling back the delicate thin meat over the forehead with all the care in the world.

Disco Christening

When Keith Pearson phoned the Cawdor Bay Hotel (***AA) to book a reception after Owen Peredur's christening, he was asked if he wanted to arrange a disco afterwards. A disco? He was assured by the manager, whose voice had the consistency of molasses, that it was all the rage, people loved it. Abso-lute-ly loved it! He explained. After the formality, the lace-lined palaver and the vows before God and the godparents, you needed to be able to let your hair down. Shake it on down, Mr Pearson. Shake it on down! The manager sounded as if he'd been taking lots of drugs.

It was unfortunate that Aunt Higgy passed away the week before the christening. Dove & Son, the undertakers who always buried the Pearsons, had a bit of a rush on, what with the flu outbreak and a virulent attack of MRSA which picked off a dozen old people in Prince William Hospital in two days. So they could only bury Higgy on the same Sunday. And because her second cousin twice removed, Bessie Pearson, was one of those scythed off by the influenza, Mr Dove, always the most compassionate man, offered a two-for-one deal, where Aunt Higgy would be “looked after” along with someone else, thereby halving the costs.

The other dearly-departed was a lonely spinster, so they wouldn’t need an extra car for the mourners. As it transpired they didn’t even need one car, as nobody bothered to go. Each family member paid their share of the funeral arrangements, which, given the number of the tribe, reduced each contribution to a round twenty quid. Consciences salved, the Pearsons as an entity felt pleased they had played a small part in the send-off. Even if there was no-one there to actually send her off into the beyond, or heaven, or wherever.

Aunt Higgy wasn’t well thought of. She kept her love in an iron container at the bottom of the septic tank so it was little surprise that, given the choice, everyone chose to go to the christening. She had irradiated a smoldering hatred of all and sundry and all and sundry had at the very least disliked her in return.

The child to be baptised, Owen Peredur Pearson, radiated cherubic innocence and contentment. He had survived an illness in the first few weeks of his life that had almost stolen him away and his bloated pasty face had actually been taking the penultimate gasp of air when he pulled back from the brink. His traumatised parents were told that he had probably choked on something unbeknown to them but the shock of being on the brink of death had dislodged it just as invisibly. ‘It happens,’ said the doctor with a professional shrug, the shrug that signals ‘I can’t get involved in your pain or I won’t be able to play golf tomorrow.’

Owen was trebly precious for that and even his

brother and sister didn't grudge him the limitless attention he got from his mother from that day on. They recognised that protective, maternal mix of fear and care as something that might come in useful in their own lives later on, something to invest in.

That awful night, as she cradled her barely sentient son, Anne Pearson had glimpsed her child in the limbo puerorum, the purgatorial half-way house where un-baptised children go. It's a white room with a white wall and a white door and there are no comforts beyond the company of the other terrified kids who will also be trapped there forever.

The day of the christening dawned with a strange lilac light coming out of the east, which was soon dissipated by a confident sun. Keith and his wife Anne woke first thing, as excited as could be.

Despite the family antipathy, Keith and Anne felt they should mark the old lady's passing in some reverential way, so after a conflab with the family elders – Uncle Turk, the Duchess and Minging Pete – they held a minute's silence in the disco.

To keep the men at the bar happy, this coincided with half-time in the Premiership football game, so the men posed respectfully with their lagers in front of the TV while the children, in frozen, mannequin poses, nodded their heads groundwards, as if in prayer, in a break from Boney M.

'She'd have liked that,' said Keith.

'She didn't like anything, Keith,' said Anne, nodding to the barman that he could turn up the volume on the telly again.

'Oh, she wasn't that bad.'

'She was entirely bad. What about that time she taught all the children to do that obscene gesture?'

'Which obscene gesture?' Embarrassingly, Anne formed her fingers into an exaggerated 'O' and pressed her tongue inside, waggling it about.

'The international suggestion of cunnilingus, Keith. We had parents in tears when they came to pick up the kids. One of the children repeated it in the nativity play, in the direction of the three wise men. That woman came to family gatherings just so she could sabotage them. She almost brought this family to its knees on more than one occasion, she really did. And what about the really bad stuff? I'll just mention one of her crimes against the family, shall I? What about the time she paid a man to kill her cousin's dog? It was hanged, Keith, and all because Higgy didn't like the way it yapped.'

'She belonged to a different generation. They had to be tough to survive. The war tempered them like steel.'

'I appreciate that this is a day when we're meant to forgive but she was beyond the pale. She was a spiteful, vindictive, miserly, hurtful woman, with a heart of ice.'

'Come on, say what you think. Don't hold back now.'

Anne did laugh at that. She had gone an adjective too far.

And that would have been that. Except for another adjective that would have stuck as appropriately to Higgie as a bluebottle to flypaper. Scheming.

Had she attended the christening, Higgie would have attentively noted how sallow Christine looked and how ill-behaved Tracey's twins were as they ricocheted their way around the aisles and how Tracey's mother's hair was such a shocking shade of bottle orange that she looked like a woman knitting at the base of the guillotine. She would have seen how Sian and Thomas' marital drift had now taken them so far apart that they were out of each other's hailing reach. Even as they held hands she'd have seen how it was just an automatic reflex, and they would barely have felt each other's warmth.

Higgie scorned so many of them, this pathetic dynasty which had bred too many brats and eaten too much fat. She despised the soulless, drab estates where they lived and their way of measuring success by the newness of their car registrations and the price tags of their designer spectacles. They didn't want for anything, yet they craved more. They were soft and gutless as a family and she was ashamed to be of their ilk. That they were soft, yes, that was their greatest sin and the reason they would be punished. The men's hands were feeble, unaccustomed to a single day's real work. Hands like white Play-Doh, bloodless and marmoreal. And those palpy bottom lips, that were handed on as genetic collateral from one generation to the next that made them shower spittle at one another when they talked! Foul people!

Higgy. This rebarbative woman had plotted how she would act from beyond the grave long before her body packed in. Long before the countdown sequence started, the organs shutting down in order of increasing importance, through kidneys to liver and on finally to the systolic and anastolic pulses of the heart, she was all the while planning her attack on the family. In Al Qaeda parlance it would be a spectacular.

She's been diagnosed with Parkinson's a few weeks after everyone else had come to the conclusion that she was suffering from it. The tell-tale stare, the awkward gait. When they heard it confirmed they greeted the news with as much compassionate warmth toward her as they could, which wasn't enough to revive a frozen dormouse.

After the diagnosis, Higgy knew exactly what to do. She arranged a meeting with Maindee, the devil's own solicitor, and asked her two helpmates Maurice and Clitheroe to meet her at his office. One used to work in a tie shop but now ran a care home called the Hollies. Clitheroe was a farm worker whose leg had been crushed after being pinned down by a falling tractor when ploughing. The farmer had been too mean to wait until the wet earth had dried enough after some heavy rain to make it safe to work on the steeply raked camber of the Upper Field.

As scumbag solicitors go, Maindee came from the bottom of the vat full of suppurating vileness where solicitors come to dine like flies. He was a man who robbed people of their inheritances, twisting a fine legal mind to bent purpose.

She told Maindee she wanted to give Maurice and Clitheroe twenty thousand pounds each, along with a further twenty for expenses. He could take ten for his troubles and the remainder, after the sale of the house, was to go to the Jehovah's Witnesses, and for his share Maindee was entrusted to make sure that this was made as public within the family as possible. They all hated the Witnesses. Maindee smiled in that pantomime unctuous way of his, and said he would accede to all her wishes.

Over the next few months Maurice and Clitheroe, who were getting a conventional wage from her in addition to the money promised in the will, contacted a lot of specialist suppliers and importers, and as their net was cast ever wider, they started to contact shadier and more duplicitous fellows who could buy increasingly endangered or dangerous species. Her secret plan was very much in train. They bought glass cages for arriving stock and Higgy marked out a feeding regime – mainly of rats and mice – in a black ledger, which she kept scrupulously up to date, as if it were a way of keeping her memory intact.

They bought poisonous snakes from all continents: corals and coppermouths and rattlesnakes of all kinds, diamondback, timber, sidewinder and the most serious of all – the aggressive Mojave rattler. Higgy loved tapping her fingers on the glass in the cage in the cellar to stir him up. He lunged directly at the glass as if it could head butt its way out. Their contacts in Asia got them cobras of all lengths and dispositions: seemingly languid king cobras that could rear up in a flash, and Egyptian cobras so lethal that minutes after a bite necrosis was sure to set in, the skin of the victim turning into a spreading, dark contusion as the cells simply died away. In the back bedroom there was the fearless ferde-lance which attacked quite without provocation and then speedier serpents such as the black mamba and the bushmaster. Her house slithered.

The ledger took note of each arrival, giving marks out of five for innate aggression and general state of health. But the animals that took pride of place among all her reptiles were the top five dangerous snakes of Australia, the top five most dangerous snakes in the world. The inland Taipan, five out of five. The Eastern brown snake, not much to look at, but another certain five. And full marks too to the peninsula tiger and the mainland tiger. Venomous, chilling, angry. They would certainly do the trick. How she hated her family, especially as her illness took hold of her and her resentment of their collective health grew like topsy.

But the snake buying activity accelerated the decaying effect of her illness and she died, as everyone had predicted, entirely alone.

So she missed out on key events in her body's passage through the closing chapter of her life. That would have really upset her spirit. If she'd been able to lie down next to the coffin and hitch a lift to her own funeral she'd been puzzled not to see any other cars making up the cortege. Behind her own vehicle was the hearse taking Bessie, who'd looked terrible before they slapped on a bit of makeup, bringing some colour to her chalk-white cheeks. She lay there on the slab like a turkey that had been stretched on the rack by a medieval torturer, her legs as white as bone.

They got to the church and by now she wouldn't have just been offended. It wasn't even St. Saviour's, where she'd been as a girl, but rather a modern box of a place in the middle of the crematorium grounds, which was just the sort of place she hated. Had she been there she would have been agonisingly angry, vowing that she would wreak revenge for this slight on her memory. But all that was arranged, conveniently enough. Maurice and Clitheroe would see to that. They would allow her to express the whole spectrum of spite.

It had once mattered to be a Pearson: a playground slight against a younger member of the clan would bring down the wrath of the other Pearson children who would be as avenging angels, scrapping dervishes in the dust of the yard. In one such attack a bullying lad had actually had his leg broken by two Pearson siblings as they pulled in different directions.

And they would stand together in other matters as well and even Higgy would not stand for anyone to say a bad thing about any one of them, even though she would vent her spleen about them herself at the drop of a hat. She said such horrible things that sometimes the family would have an away day at the seaside or at a country park when they would try to purge themselves of all the half-lies, untruths, slurs and brickbats Higgy had unleashed as a swarm of attacking bacteria against them.

At the church entrance the two men deftly manhandled the first coffin onto a trolley and rolled it in front of the pine pews. Her own coffin followed, a cheap affair with imitation brass handles and small wreath on top with a label which said noncommittally: 'In our thoughts. The Pearson family.'

The officiating minister sped briskly through the brief biographies. Higgy merited some ninety seconds in total. Her full name. Where she was born. How she had been a staunch attendee at Rehoboth chapel before it was sadly knocked down to make way for the new by-pass. It described her as a backbone of the Pearson family and, just as he said that, one of them arrived in the otherwise empty church. Mark Pearson, one of the nephews she despised the most, a gracile weasel of man with sharp little teeth to match. She would have known why he was here, drawn by the possibility of her dying intestate. Little did Mark know that she had left everything, including the silver and china, to the Witnesses. One of them, a cross-eyed woman called Letitia, had brought her a copy of *The Watchtower* every week for four years and had asked for nothing more than considering their way to God. She knew that would put the cat among the pigeons. It would put a starving Siberian tiger right in the loft.

Mark felt a pneumonic chill running through his body and imagined cold lips pressing against the part of his collarbone that was visible through the shirt. Higgy's anger would have become incendiary rage when the minister pressed a button and her body was summarily consigned to the flames! A crematorium! She would have been furious beyond speech or action. Higgy'd made sure that every one Jack of them knew she wanted to be interned with all the rest of the family. This final slight would have been the last straw, which made the revenge she would never actually taste all the more sweet.

The velvet curtains closed on her coffin and slid along the rollers to the flames. Greedy Mark went out to the car. He was so eager to leave he forgot to acknowledge the minister who held out a consoling hand to a man whose head was full of speculative figures about Higgy's house and how many ways they had to divvy up the cash. He was almost the nearest relative to her.

The disco would have upset her almost as much as seeing her body being burned and her ashes scooped up on a long handled shovel and put in the sort of plastic bag you used when carrying a goldfish back from the fair. The screeching, unfamiliar music was a chimpanzee cacophony resonating in her cranium. On the neat parquet dance floor were four generations of Pearsons, entirely unaware of the fate that was to befall them. Dancing to the Gap band and Showadywaddy, Shakin Stevens and Meatloaf. And a few more up-to-date numbers. Madonna duetting with Justin Timberlake.

Her henchmen took the bulging bin sacks and hauled them up the steps of the hotel kitchens and into the ballroom. Score settling was their unbridled delight.

The D.J. was animatedly encouraging everybody to get on down, and even the boozers from the sports bar drifted in when they heard the opening bars of Michael Jackson's 'Thriller'. He might be a one-man freak show but he made some of the most danceable music this side of Burundi.

On a nod from Maurice, Clitheroe opened each of

the straining bin sacks and shook out the writhing, spitting contents on the floor. The animals slithered and reared and coiled and spat and hissed and bit. Adults and children scattered in all directions but many couldn't get over the metallic arc of the balustrade that hemmed them in on two sides and the panic sent many of them crashing into each other. Some of the snakes were already out in the hotel reception and others were climbing up the indoor trellis work.

A king cobra, hood fully extended on the longest neck, reared up next to a yucca plant, ready to pick off anyone foolish enough to stray within range. Some snakes struck out at other snakes even as Maurice and Clitheroe were driving off in their white van, smugly satisfied that not one of them had been attacked as they dumped them all out. Maurice had already been bitten by a mamba in Higgy's basement and it had been touch-and-go whether the anti-venom would work in time.

The hotel manager gabbled words down the phone after dialing nine-nine-nine and had to be persuaded to stop saying the word "snakes" over and over and calm down so he could explain which service was needed. All of them, he babbled. Snakes!

The D.J. had the worst time of it, mainly because of the potted olive trees that hemmed in his booth in the corner. Some of the arboreal snakes had immediately gravitated upwards, and he had to fend them off with the sleeves of his precious Northern soul records. He batted a mamba with a really rare copy of Tommy Navarro's 'I Cried My Life Away'.

When he was about twelve years of age Owen Peredur's favourite family story was about the sacks full of snakes someone had unleashed on his christening. They were ever so lucky no-one got seriously hurt, for even though two people were bitten, they both survived to tell the tale, as did the RSPCA inspector who sealed off the hotel and caught the serpents one by one with his pair of special tongs. Forty eight in total.

Owen particularly liked the image of his redoubtable auntie Lil beating away a fearsome rattlesnake with her walking stick, beating it back all the way to the cloakroom where a terrified attendant had become incontinent with fear as a coppermouth snake appeared behind the rack of coats and opened its terrifying gape. Lil was indomitable, she really was, as was the whole family. After a Biblical onslaught of snakes they really could cope with just about anything. He underlined his surname on the front of his school exercise book. Pearson. A strong name. Full of character. The sort of stuff that stood you in good stead when life was all chill wind and challenge. He wanted to be like Lil. He would be.

Nighthawks

The session down the job centre had not gone too well. The man behind the Plexiglass screen hadn't liked Planer's jokes and had put him down as a flippant time-waster, which could really scupper his benefit payments.

'I'm afraid we can't accommodate any one of your three preferred career options,' – Planer had expressed a desire to be an ocarina salesman, pearl diver and glider pilot – 'and so I'm afraid you'll have to look at something less, well, exotic.'

Planer didn't even get the chance to explain about the man from Senegal who'd shared digs with him when they were both working on the M4. Salif showed him how to make three kinds of ocarina and it was a life skill Planer carried with him: how to fashion the transverse, the pendant and the inline and get rare good sounds out of all of them.

At forty-nine Planer had acquired a range of skills. He described himself as a willing hand, but there was raging unemployment and no need for any hands. Lines formed even for menial work and dirty tasks.

The surly man gave him a print-out of job vacancies

in the area and it was a demeaning list. In the old days he'd have lumped them all in the category marked 'skivvy'. There were a few catering jobs and a desirable career option as an assistant lavatory attendant in the Scrumballs Terrace conveniences, which actually had a pension scheme attached as if he might choose to grow old and retire in the fetid bunker, in the smell of other people's insides.

'You're kidding me, right?'

'No one jests in this job, Mr Planer. We're civil servants.'

'And if I refuse all of these?'

'The State would, I'm afraid, take a dim view. Let me suggest the job at the abattoir. "Meat Excavator". We haven't had many enquiries about that. It seems most of the long term unemployed in this area have become vegetarian overnight.'

So Planer caught the Number 61 bus to a huge concrete bunker on the edge of town. A smoke stack plumed the smell and smuts high into the air. His job interview was perfunctory. He was shown where to clock in and given his overalls and boots. Disposable caps came from a dispenser.

'You'll find it hard at first. There's a damn sight too much blood for most people, but we won't ask you to work the stun gun in your first few weeks. We'll just let you get the hang of it. But I would say be very careful when walking around – the floors are very slippery as one of the sluice channels has clogged and it'll take a few days to get it running again.'

He pointed at a mound of innards and offal

which were being pushed into a corner by a gangling Rastafarian wielding an U-shaped rubber brush.

By the afternoon Planer was already wielding the stun gun, the iron bolt shooting into the animal's skull with such precise force that it would have dropped down stone dead were it not pinioned by the metal sides of the killing harness. He worked in a fine mist of blood which came off the lancing and cutting tools from the other men on the line. He counted fifty animals in and, as he left at the end of his first shift, saw four lorries moving carcasses out of the goods yard.

Planer had a shower after reaching the flat and then walked down to the Drovers' where he was due to meet Henry. He was never seen in daylight for medical reasons; a rare condition which banished him from sunlight. Henry danced like a God.

His friend was swimming away from himself into a lagoon of worry, full of gin. On the bar stool he was exposed, open to view and judgmental scrutiny.

'That'll have to be the last one,' said the barman, 'or I won't have enough gin to sell to my sober customers.'

'Indubitably,' said Henry.

Henry was fighting two phobias: phengophobia, a fear of daylight and soberphobia, a fear of seeing the world without the blur of alcohol. Booze. It was a hazy, necessary cordon sanitaire separating him from the monsters and howling voices. A night-owl by necessity, he used to work in the casino and slept in the staff room, an indulgence granted him by the Chinese managers because he'd always volunteer to do the extra hours, even when tacked on the end of a killer shift.

Planer put a bag of meat on the counter in front of him: his friend was about to embark on a high protein diet.

'I hear you've taken a job in the killing fields,' said Henry, with a pantomime slur.

'It was the only career path left – other than a lavatory cleaner.'

'I'm not allowed any more hooch here I'm afraid,' said Henry, waving a limp wrist in the direction of the barman, who gave them both a genuinely benign smile.

'So let's go do what we do best.'

Planer and Henry had been given a spare key to the ice rink and even when Henry was seven sheets to the wind he could still dance better than anyone: he levitated in air, took space as a challenge and could skate out of his body. He was a genius on skates and had trained in Helsinki and Leningrad. His element was frozen water.

They let themselves in through the back door, went straight up into the arena and turned on the rink lights using a dimmer. Henry fell over twice before they got to the guard rail but then lifted himself up again, expressing a Falstaffian fart.

Planer loved the incongruity of it all – how this barely articulate dipsomane could rouse himself from near torpor to delicious flight. The man wobbled when he walked, for Christ's sake!

They had stashed their skates behind a fire hose in a cupboard. Henry had a spangly pair with blades he had made himself using an industrial grinder. Planer had chunky, utilitarian ones, which made him feel safe when he had to catch Henry.

Henry and Planer went up to the control booth and slipped in a CD of music that Henry had made. It had the dark majesty of Gorecki's 'Three Pieces in Olden Style' along with some pulsating dance anthems from Faithless. Henry took the music mixes seriously as he required the shock of the new to lift his skating game. And he loved Faithless: he always included something by them. It kept him young. Bugger being forty-eight.

It took Henry a few clumsy minutes to lace his skates as the music on the CD started to spread a grey cloak of mordant music across the glister. The Gorecki: no laughs, but lots of lingering beauty. He took a few faltering steps before his innate grace kicked in and he started to do some warm-up loops, seeming to lose weight as he did so. Planer went counter-clockwise to him, the strangeness of the music vexing him as his mind tried to pick out a rhythm or create an image he could fix on. He saw clouds of dark steam coming off the stacks of a steelworks and ragged lines of refugees coming out of the forest. Planer had seen things that had burned into his memory in Burundi, El Salvador and Guatemala. The music triggered flashbacks to a childhood in the shadow of the coking ovens and his peregrinating work as a photographer.

Henry, meanwhile, was vividly alive in the moment, working up the synchronised rhythm of breathing and movement, looking for cues in the music to which he could respond. He had dismissed the slowdown effects of the alcohol and had found fluid elegance in his motion.

In the shadow of a pillar, in the topmost tier of

the seating area, a young film student called Kyle trained his PD 150 camera on the two men. He'd heard rumours about them sufficient for him to get permission from the rink owner to keep watch. The owner himself was intrigued: two old guys who broke in to figure-skate. A cleaner had seen them once, he'd said they danced pretty well.

As the beats started pounding out from the speakers Planer reckoned the music was too loud and feared they were going to get caught, but Henry said he needed to feel the bass notes in his diaphragm.

He started with easy jumps, working incrementally through the doubles, the triples and the quads as Planer started to work up speed in his counter-loops.

Thirty years earlier, Henry's father, when he heard his son was thinking of taking up figure-skating full time, broke his son's wrist by crunching it against the brick edge of the back door frame. Henry was gutted. It was three days before his audition for the Mariposa School of Skating in Barrie, Ontario. Ringing them to let them know he wasn't coming for the audition was one of the lowest points of his life. He drank to forget that precise moment and to drown his anger at his dad. An anger he sometimes failed to control. Once he had smashed his fist into Planer's face because he dropped him in mid-mazurka. So Henry tried to drown his anger just as much as he tried to forget his father. But skating, well, that was his sublime revenge.

Planer realised there was something different about this night when Henry swooped past him and executed a leap that he had never ever seen before, a sort of vulture swoop that saw his partner hurl himself forward, almost as if he was going to take a tumble before righting himself. Planer enjoyed this clownish mock-clumsiness. With Swiss precision Planer sent him skywards with a flick of both wrists. Henry seemed to beat gravity as he flew in a forty foot arc, to land as sure-footedly as a chamois goat.

They gyred towards the middle; now back to a programmed routine: the first complicated move, where Planer threw him in the air and Henry managed to spin both ways in one single flight, truly seemed to defeat the laws of physics. On impact, his skates splintered the ice into a million shards. Planer slowed down momentarily, just enough to be on the very cusp of moving and stopping. He needed to give his friend a hurling lift straight up into the air so that Henry was airborne above Planer's head and shoulders, having enough height to close his legs and give the impression he was going to cleave his friend's head in two as the skates came down. And then, with just a nanosecond to spare, he opened them again and did the splits, landing squarely on Planer's nonplussed bonce. It was William Tell's arrow, the circus knife-thrower's cutting edge.

Planer imagined how the crowds would be wowed by this audacious feat. He then bowed his head so Henry could tumble forward, but that bit didn't go to plan. Henry was physically sick, projectile vomiting of the first order. He seemed uncertain on his legs at that point and quite unaware that he had made skating history: executing a move that even the mighty Rondel for all his innate muscularity and verve had failed to do, and without killing Planer in the bargain. Planer had to help his friend take off his skates and clean up the mess. He splashed out on a cab to get them home. Henry wore shades and smelled of juniper from the earlier gin. He looked older by a decade.

The next morning, while Planer and Harry slept off their exertions, Kyle showed the rink manager, Phil Hurt, the footage: two middle-aged men making magic happen. Hurt knew before they even got to the near-decapitation that he was looking at one of the best skaters in the world.

'I'd like to put this stuff online,' said Kyle, 'just to see what happens.'

'With my blessing,' said Hurt, eager to know more about the back story.

The video on YouTube became the most watched item in the world. And they were sought for, hunted high and low until they gave themselves up to celebrity. They appeared on *Jonathan Ross*, and a serialised account of their lives was printed in *The Daily Mail*. They were feted, toasted and lauded. Henry enjoyed the free drinks as he careered from TV studio to photo-shoot to magazine interview in limousines with tinted windows. Pepsi got in touch, so did a gaggle of clothes manufacturers. They could have their own lines; hell, they could have their own shops. For Henry, all the buzz and attention simply worked up a thirst.

Planer insisted on carrying on in work. He liked the men he worked with. When Planer got to work on the Wednesday a phalanx of photographers snapped away near the security booth. Inside, there was an eerie hush about the place and more eerie still when

Trevor Bunley, one of the Bunley Brothers who owned the place, came up to him as he clocked in. The man, whose complexion most resembled one of his own hung-for-21-days hunks of beef, took him by the arm and led him past two lines of his fellow abattoirees into Cutting Room Three, which was the biggest in the place. Planer couldn't believe his eyes. They'd replaced the blood-bespattered cement floor with a perfect sheet of ice, and had even installed hand rails around the walls.

'So you can practice lunchtimes, and we can watch.'

As his workers applauded this briefest of speeches, Planer's eyes spotted the spectator stand on one edge. The chippies at the abattoir had worked at a frenzied lick to get them built and had even draped them with bunting. Cued by a nod from Trevor, one of the ladies from the canteen stepped forward and gave Planer a pair of skates, sporting a Bunleys-for-Beef slogan and motifs of flying sausages and burgers. Planer had to laugh.

'Just what I always wanted,' said Planer to much applause, which resounded around the chill room until he put on his skates and took to the ice. He executed a perfect mazurka as he sang along to a routine he'd perfected in his head but had never actually danced. As he went ever faster, he sang one of his favourite hymns, and he might have been giving theme the keys of the kingdom, he really could, because they were all as quiet as field mice, all ninety five employees in their Cliniwhite hats, as they watched him work his way through his alphabet of moves.

When Planer walked into the bar to meet Henry that night, a palpable buzz of excitement tingled its way around the room. There was a starburst of paparazzi flashbulbs and there were an awful lot of strangers in the place. Henry was drinking Perrier.

'We've been invited to represent the UK in the world championships. No trials, no competitions, just a straight entry based on the strength of what we've done in the past,' said Henry, without ceremony. He sipped, with distaste.

'Blimey, no wonder you're on the weak stuff. When are they?'

'In two weeks' time.'

'You'll be needing something a little stronger then?'

'I most certainly will.'

They trained down at the abattoir where Planer now just worked half days. The company loved having the television crews coming back and forth and gave them all free samples and hot beef baguettes.

Getting Henry into the place involved using cars with actual curtains on the windows and changing clocks so that he never actually saw that it was daytime, enough of a ruse to confuse his phobia. He still got nervous if he simply heard the word 'day'.

For a couple of days they had a skating coach, Jurek, to help them but all he could do, despite years of training Lithuanians, was watch the two of them achieve things they shouldn't be able to. Their levels of fitness were laughably low.

The two men worked out a dynamite routine, weaving together Asian dub beats and old war movie themes, helped along by Planer's nephew who was a DJ and record producer. He added some Stravinsky and some psychedelic beats from Togo and Benin from the 1970s. Henry loved these in particular as they had the madcap energy of people who were clearly out of their boxes, and he was no stranger to that state. He drank Chartreuse from plastic cups by way of training.

The fateful day dawned in Reykjavik. Planer felt awkward in his new costume, but not as awkward as Henry, who found it clingy around the capaciousness of his behind.

Russia and Denmark were the countries to watch, both countries backed by the tipsters and the bookmakers right up until Planer and Henry threw their hats into the ring, or into the rink, rather. On the night flight to Iceland the Nighthawks, as they now styled themselves, had chatted amiably about the challenge ahead. They talked about Miles Davis and Shakespeare and other people who had pushed the boat out into new and open water. Henry held back from the booze and resisted the free drinks, a token gesture really as he'd already sunk a good few in the airport bar.

Henry limbered up with a couple of Goldschlagers and two quick turns around the ice of the practice rink. He felt a little queasy as if he were coming down with something. He'd been listening to the music over and over, as had Planer, who knew every note and nuance. They both put on their black spandex costumes and their new skates. They were smiling as they went through the doors into the cinema show of their performance, a capacity crowd on its feet the moment they stepped into the glare.

Deafening cheers – not least from the hundred abattoir workers who had made the trip – followed them as they went around the rink in increasingly decreasing figures of eight. They wove a pattern into each other with delicious speed, two men as a loom of motion.

Their first few moves were perfectly executed and in any other pair's routine would have been climactic: perfect pirouettes, explosive bursts of energy and synchronicity, but they skated with all the verve of chefs calmly arranging their ingredients. The crowd in the arena knew this; so too did the huge worldwide television audience as Henry worked up a panting sweat and started to accelerate into the pièce de résistance.

He was travelling too fast and was mentally too far into the move to notice the pains radiating into his body or to register the heart seizure which convulsed him in mid air, so that people thought this was all part of the act. He was dead before his still upright body careened towards the judging panel.

There's one photograph that sums up what happened: a shot taken by an enterprising photographer who had squeezed beneath the judges table. It showed a row of limp clenched fists, like white tulips, holding onto the numbers they would have shortly held aloft, ones and noughts in repeating order, showing they would have given the 'Hawks' every available point, had not Henry died in mid routine, becoming the first ever martyr of the ice.

Planer never found another partner, but enjoyed

his return to the meat factory. Normality was welcome after the blur of attention which followed Henry's death. On a good day Planer would remember their arabesques as he carved the Uruguayan beef with the file saw. And he could conjure up Henry's smile as his teeth flashed in orbit.

Mission Creep

Krink was the only contract killer working out of Gwynedd. Despite his stranglehold on the market – and how telling was that word when you considered his favoured modus operandi – he made a poor fist of it, with only two hits to his name these past three years and one of those was just a quick nudge for a rich old man over a cliff near Colwyn Bay. It made him glum, and as he stared at the brown sludge of coffee in the chipped mug on the café table he tried to banish the blues. It wasn't easy. His bank account had dwindled, what with takings from the bookshop being down and people clearly cutting back on their assassination budgets.

This part of north Wales was a thinly populated place, with a landscape of jagged dragons' teeth and high sheep folds and just as the population was a trifle spare so too was the criminal underworld that shadowed it, confined to a few sheep stealers and the usual drug traders from the estates in Liverpool who sped along the A55 in their pimp-my-ride BMWs, each a gleaming wonderland of chrome, tinted windows and multi-layer paint jobs. They brought C-grade skank and lower grade whizz, each cut with weed killer and flour, even brick dust sometimes, just to make the heroin look a bit more brown.

South of the coast where the land rises in its jagged dentitions were hills where only bachelor farmers lived and here on the sea's edge, along the Costa Geriatrica, many of the old grippers who lived here were only killing time, waiting for the Reaper to come and slice them out of their bath chairs.

Krink lived in one of those death towns so crammed with old folk that it actually had a bath chair shop, like a throwback to the Empire days. Horace Keel and Son still managed to ply their trade in the age of the Zimmer and the Stannah stair lift, their emporium full of raffia and moth dust. Given an onshore breeze you could stand in the middle of the High Street and smell the embalming fluid.

The café that morning was full of people in the middle of a shift change, with white hatted nightbirds who'd just finished the last batch of loaves at the nearby bakery having a quick cuppa before going to bed and shop workers fueling for the zombie-day ahead. Krink assessed each of them with a professional eye, drawn to weakness, habit and obsessive tics much as most people were attracted by beauty or style. He identified an affair in its early stages, and read the slippery body language of a shoplifter who was practicing prestidigitation on the salt and pepper shakers. Opposite him was a fat man, slobbering over a heaped bowl of breakfast linguine alla vongole. The man was a quivering, heavy-breathing icon of greed. He couldn't get the pasta into his mouth fast enough. A slinky psychopath, adept with piano wire, could work wonders for his table manners. A rivulet of tomato sauce ran down the man's neck, resembling a garrote victim. Krink's fingers tensed at the thought...

Krink noticed a tiny flash of light in the street, tell tale sunlight refracted off the curve of a camera lens. Special Branch must be snapping him from the van. He had been followed once or twice that month – all the result of a computer glitch which had put him on the sex offenders' register – but he saw it as a training exercise and no matter how many times they found where he was he could always, always give them the slip, as if he had the mantle of invisibility to drape over his shoulders. He'd hacked into the police mainframe to find out why he was under surveillance and knew he could delete all knowledge of himself if he so desired. They'd taken so many photographs of him that he felt like a male model, despite his pipe-cleaner frame and bulbous eyes with their bags of tiredness underneath and the thinness of his blonde wisps of hair. All in all it was a face with a lived-in look – a squat for a hell of a lot of hard-partying people. Most prominent of all was the teeth, the jagged feature that made him look half shark, half graveyard, a distinctive mix of tombstone molars and ferocious incisors. He borrowed some guy's red kagoule and slipped out the back door.

As he left town he checked in the rear view mirror and the unmarked car was still stationery. Krink thought, how on earth did they ever catch anyone?

The car gears squealed as he went up the one-in-nine gradient that took him past Twyn-y-Rhodyn farm. He cut through Dol Padog plantations and slalomed the car along the forestry roads until he'd gained a thousand feet and the ozone in the subalpine air made his head spin. He parked on a mossy verge at the base of the track that criss-crossed a huge expanse of bracken and headed for the snake traps.

There were forty wide-mouthed Kilner jars buried on the hillside and Krink knew he could expect to find a snake alive in at least three of them. He took out his thick gloves and a cleft hazel stick, along with a small gamekeeper's bag filled with phials and other kit and strode out into waist-high ferns. April was a good time as the snakes were still torpid after their winter's sleep. Not that they wouldn't be angry about spending a night or three in a glass prison.

The first three were full of bric-a-brac: dried fern fronds, a beetle struggling on its back, and sheep droppings. The fourth held a fear-crazed shrew that was trying to somersault its way out of the glass mouth. Krink released it and it caught its tiny breath before racing away, a mad clockwork toy heading for the hedge.

The last jar on the ridge held a fine specimen of male reptile, its colour scheme designed to shock, a waspish black and yellow-white zigzagging right the way along a meaty back down to its pin-tail. Its pipe body coiled and recoiled, restless, agitated. The walls of the jar were sufficiently curved to deny the snake any chance of escape as Krink pinioned its head between the tines of the stick. Keeping the snake in place he turned the jar, juggling it slowly so that the head was near the opening and he could do his work. The muscled body bucked and twisted but Krink kept a firm grip. He milked the venom straight into the phial as the creature's eyes stared at him and the fangs, hypodermically, dripped their stunning fluids. Then, with the head sequestered in his fist, Krink lifted out the snake and placed it on a grassy tump from where it slithered away after a few seconds of gaining composure. There were two more snakes to harvest: one a curiosity as its venom was tinged with purple, a hint of whinberries. Krink set the seal on the glass container. He labelled it Brynberllan 3. He liked to know the provenance of his bullets.

On a housing estate fifty miles away a group of women were meeting to talk about things of major import.

The eldest among them, Margot, without a silent 't', dished out some cigarettes, ultra-cheap ones which gave her a rasping cough. The cigarettes she smoked were so cheap they didn't even include tobacco, the nicotine sprayed on.

They were meeting at the community centre, although community had to be used in an ironic sense. They all lived in a sink estate where society had pulled the plug years ago. It was nowadays divided into sections, like Berlin after the war. There were the prefabs, left over from the last war and full of damp, next to the fifties houses with walls as thin as tissue. Then there was Debtor's Row, full of rent defaulters from other sink estates, who even if you set the bar for standards pretty low would limbo dance their scrotty way underneath.

The women each had a mug of very strong tea. They were addicted to caffeine just as surely as their sons and daughters were hooked on hard drugs.

Kylie was telling them how her son had rifled through her handbag and taken everything he could find, and he would even have taken her benefit cheque had she not had the foresight to hide it behind a skirting board next to the washing machine. When she'd confronted him he'd been sufficiently cooked on something to try to stare her down. Coolly she told him she was asking him to leave the house until he was clean. It was breaking her heart, she told him, but he had to learn to fend for himself on the street, and that would break him or make him.

The first time she had found drugs in his possession she knew nothing about them, where they came from, what you did with them. But like all the mothers on the estate she'd been forced to learn, playing catch up with her little boy turning man. By now he was shooting up ketamine between his toes, the rest of his veins pushed to collapse. When you were getting your highs from horse tranquilisers, bottom wasn't far away. Little wonder that they had convened to work out a way of ridding Llwyngog estate of the plague.

All of the drugs trade on the estate was handled by a group of men who loved violence and Nazi Germany and were so feared that even the police stayed clear. There was something almost supernatural about the evil that emanated from them and the house on the estate which they had commandeered. One day, reckoned the local police superintendent, peering at the future through a fug of smoke from his Bensons, they would have enough evidence to take in a fleet of marias, take in the Army in tanks if necessary and haul them all in for a kicking in the cells. But the dealers wove such a web of fear that it was hard to isolate someone who would squeal. The women knew this, and it was the principal reason they made the call to a man who knew a man who knew another man who knew how to leave a message for Krink.

It was no better a life than Krink's, although Kamosiwe's appearance in his life gave it a new and strange dimension – a sidekick, a confidante, maybe even a friend. Up until their serendipitous meeting Krink had been the very apogee of loneliness, who often had to refresh his social skills by reading Victorian novels, where people greet and meet a lot. It wasn't often you met a Yanomamo Indian, let's face it, certainly not in Llandudno Junction, where they'd found themselves sharing a table at Real Fried Chicken and Krink had been stumped by the man's accent when he'd ordered himself a bucket of chicken pieces, and was prompted to ask about it. Kamosiwe had an easy manner and his arm muscles had a powerful sheen. He was an attractive man.

Krink thought it strange how quickly he'd found himself confiding in him. It might have been the huge differences in their outlooks; it might have been the great similarities that can bind two absolute strangers in next to no time if given half a human chance. Or it might be that it was a time to unburden, to prepare for that later reckoning that if he'd had a vestige of faith, other than a basic fear of the void beyond, might have vexed him a bit more than it did. Krink smiled at the thought of his new friend, almost with a sexual frisson, and wondered why he'd let his guard slip so readily. Normally he thought of friendship as a weakness.

Krink drew down the blinds and then walked outside to pull down the metal shutters. They had only recently been sprayed by two rival gangs – The World Security Council and the 24:7s. He would given them a fright one of these days, sure as eggs is eggs, sure as daisy. But not tonight. Tonight was for harvesting the houseplants.

Keeping a dark pharmacy of poisons right out in the open seemed to him a masterstroke. Few people knew how many of them yielded poisons and fewer still would guess how it easy it was, with the most rudimentary of lab apparatus to distill the sappy juices into delivery systems for nephritis, blindness, nerve spasm and death.

The shadows gathered under the leaves of angel's wings and a mighty Swiss cheese plant, *monstera deliciosa.* His collection was by now pretty exhaustively put together – flamingo lilies and kaffir lilies, crotons and dumb canes, poinsettias and philodendrons. Mixed in with innocuous plants of course, a little floral dressing in his deadly arbor.

He lit the small methylated spirits burner, the ghostly blue light of the flames above the wide wick reflecting on the pregnant curves of the thick amaryllis bulb which lay on the chopping board. He cut through it with dispatch, his fingers animated like a puppeteer. He then started the process that would yield pretty high grade lycorine – not a deadly poison but one which could make someone very, very ill, enough to regret each next breath. He thought of the yobs who had spray-canned his shop and imagined how his next guinea pigs, for a drop of two of tincture injected into a six pack of lagers left as if dropped accidentally, might wear hooded fleece and backward-facing baseball caps. He might adulterate a whole case of bottled beers with it, leave it somewhere obvious for their delectation and his delight.

The liquids vaporised and condensed three times. He had faith in the rituals of the old alchemists, like his great-great-great-uncle Morgan Llwyd ap Gruffudd ap Fychan, the presiding genius over a mid Wales court so ancient that even the Welsh – with their astonishing regard for such things – could not remember its origins. Whenever Morgan experimented – working on his thesis that gold was an alloy of lead and copper, a metallic marriage that could be sundered by the right acid under the right conditions – he swore by doing everything three times. *Tri chynnig i Gymro*, went the old proverb. Three tries for a Welshman. Krink trusted the clarity of his ancestor's vision. You probably do see things more clearly through one good eye. Morgan's experiments had claimed the other.

Warming to the exactitude of his task Krink prepared a noxious cocktail – crown of thorns, Jerusalem cherry and devil's backbone, mashed and juiced, cooked up and cooled down. *Tri chynnig i wenwynwr*. And three for the poisoner.

Having transferred the liquid into a pipette he then filled dinky serum phials with the pale amber liquid. He took three pieces of fresh chicken liver from the fridge and walked out into the night to do some field trials.

Vaulting the iron gates at the top end of the park, he enjoyed the jasmine tang of the June night. A hedgehog bustled along the edge of the rose garden, intent on insects. Krink crouched down behind the wall that abutted the terrace of houses and injected the liver with poison. He then walked away into the cover of a copse from where he trained his infra-red binoculars. He estimated that it would take two minutes for the first moggie to slink in and even though the first animal was ten seconds late it gave Krink some satisfaction that he'd pretty much worked out how long it would take for the molecules of liver scent to drift and scatter on the slow breeze. It was a bloated tom with a fat testicular swagger that realised that there was more than one piece of meat, its body vacillating with indecision. It struck out to the left, towards the largest piece and hunkered down to enjoy this unexpected midnight snack. 'Four seconds,' murmured Krink as he saw the first torn-off chunk slide down the epiglottis. Then the cat's whole frame seemed as if it would explode. It spasmed and died. Krink reckoned that ten times the dose and a human would be French bread in twenty seconds. Another cat shadowed its way across the grass. Krink didn't bother watching this one. He'd done enough open-air animal lab for one night.

In his dreams he flew with shearwaters, his animal familiars, across an ocean, when a huge gale threw them skywards like crackled paper above a bonfire. Birds scattergunned topsy-turvily in all directions and after what seemed liked an aeon of being storm-tossed, sometimes turned upside down by the strength of the wind, Krink found himself above an ice cap. Beneath him there were caterpillar tracks in the snow and as the Krink-bird started to drop through the air because of exhaustion he saw the ridged hump of a research station. As luck would have it, his feathered body crumpling into a snow drift, a Norwegian geologist was passing by and came over to pick up this little bird so much like an albatross and pushed it down within the warm fleece lining of his parka coat. When Krink woke, shivering, it was not from the memory of the arctic temperature but rather from the image of being cupped with great tenderness between two gloved hands.

You can tell the house where the neo-Nazis live because they've got a big graffito on the front wall proclaiming allegiance to Combat 19. In the front garden – if you can use the term for the stretch of napalmed grass where they torched a Kawasaki after an altercation with a bunch of bikers – there is a flagpole where on ceremonial occasions – such as St George's Day and Hitler's birthday – they often hoist a swastika flag. It's the one actually used by the Third Reich and if anyone has the temerity to try to bring it down they will get hurt.

The largest ground floor room of No. 3 Lavender

Drive is given over to a gym filled with homemade equipment that looks as if it came out of an Amnesty International report. One stand involves hanging upside down like a fruit bat with your belt hanging from a meat hook holding dumbbells in your hands. They have also adapted an old bedstead into a device in which you lie on the springs, while the others pile steel plates on your chest.

Today they were running a chain through the window to a tree outside and hooking it to the twin handles of an industrial-sized dustbin filled with breeze blocks and bits of brick. One of them, Scrote, was being fitted with a homemade bit for his mouth, like a scold's bridle, the sort of thing they used in medieval days to wire a woman's mouth shut.

'Take the strain, fucker,' said one gigantic man called Raz, who looked as if he could. They checked the chain was wrapped tight against the bin. And just to reassure the guinea pig the giant said. 'And if your head comes off we're going to stick it on a pole and hold you up there with pride.'

Veins stood proud on Scrote's forehead, looking fit to burst. His eyeballs looked as if they were going to jump their sockets. Out in the garden there was almost a childish glee as the ten men shouted, 'It's moving' as the bin shuddered and lifted a millimeter or so as Scrote arched his back and planted his jackboots in the damp earth. He spat out breath and drew in air, his face gurning with the difficulty of it, his skin tones running through a spectrum from crimson to claret.

'Come on fucker, bring that baby home,' shouted the

giant, his voice like bass bins in a rock sound system.

And then the bin was lifting, first with just one part of the rim still on the ground and then, accompanied with one huge exhalation like a death gasp and a great tearing sound as his knee cartilage ripped in two, Scrote started walking backwards with people clearing a path for him.

It took three of them to take the harness off Scrote's head and even the hardest man in south Wales started screaming as they did so. The men were amazed because he hadn't so much as whimpered when a schizoid who lived in of the prefabs had planted a machete in his arm. Scrote retched out two thick chunks of bone and gristle, once part of his jawbone and gums, as the men cheered to have seen something so übermensch. Four teeth kerplinked onto the gravel leaving tiny skittering trails of blood. The man washed out his mouth with tequila.

Krink watched all of this, absorbed all the data. It was always wise to know what you were up against. As Chairman Mao advised, the first condition of guerrilla warfare is the true and absolute recognition of the adversary. He'd already decided that they were in for a mix of poison and hand-to-hand combat. He'd enjoy seeing fear in the whites of their eyes. But before that could happen he had an idea about someone who might want to join him in his tasks.

In their beds the women dealt with what they'd done, going through moral contortions. One argued it was a decision born out of love, another took the Old Testament line of an eye for an eye, while others worried themselves senseless about being involved in murder. You could call it assassination, you could call it ridding the world of scum, but in the eyes of the law, and in the eye of all moral conscience, it was murder, no doubt about it. One thing they were agreed upon: if the estate was finally rid of the scum then they would have a slap up meal at The Goat, even going so far as to have starters, prawn cocktails all round.

In the sitting room above the bookshop, the two men were finishing a gargantuan breakfast.

'That was a great breakfast, Krink, although we probably had a little too much for what we're about do. It's very physical.'

Krink smiled at Kamosiwe's provocative attitude.

'And another imperative reason you should take me along is that when you were probably still asleep, dreaming of friendly nineteen year olds in crop tops and clingy skirts I ran up Crib Goch and back. I'm your fit sort of Amazonian.'

Krink suggested that he might like to come training with him, as he was just about to go out to Llanfrothen for a bit of a work-out.

They were both still feeling a little stuffed when they reached the yard and it would be a good while before the digestive juices really started to work. The old quarry site was full of rusting machines, left-overs from the days when the industry employed thousands of workers hereabouts. The engine-room door flapped open and within it jackdaws chattered manically. There was a glassy lustre to the landscape, a sheen of sunlight on the great spoil heaps, where acid rain leached through. On the surface of a nearby lake, black water shirred in the keening wind.

The trimming room was an impressive space, where dozens of men used to sit in cubicles to shape roof tiles, walling strip, whatever was required. Kamosiwe took off his top and Krink followed suit. They unwrapped the axes – two long affairs with handles of ash and blades honed to the sort of sharpness that could shave things thin enough for microscope slides. Then Kamosiwe took off his Orioles T-shirt to reveal an astonishing body painting – a leopard leaping out of the yaw of a volcano and three powerful birds of prey flying in squadron formation, one carrying a tree which looked both small and huge. Draped over that design was an exotica of feathers hanging from an elaborate necklace.

Kamosiwe told the story hidden under his shirt, he got it off his chest. 'The first creatures were the *hekura*, they are like your fairies and they live in the hills and mountains. They are very beautiful and it stands to reason that they, in turn are also attracted to beauty and so the shamans cover themselves with lovely decorations to try to attract the *hekura* into their own chests, to live there. And having a *hekura* inside you gives you power beyond measure. The volcano and the tree and the three birds are a much longer story which I could tell you over a pint sometime.'

'Are you a shaman?' asked Krink.

'In the absence of anyone else to claim the title in Llandudno Junction, I suppose I am.'

Krink laughed without causing offence. 'Thank you.'

'Thank you. I'll respect your status. But that's enough folklore studies for one morning. Let's get on with it. Show me how you can defend yourself...'

In the indian's hands the axe turned into a willow wand, a slender pliable taper which he spun around as if it operated outside of gravity's law. He struck at phantasmal men lunging away from imagined blows and parrying axe strikes. With an iron bar in his hands Krink tried a feint he'd picked up from kendo classes, many moons ago. The two men enjoyed lunging at each other, enjoyed the flashes of physical brilliance and were equally matched, Krink's experience pitted against the young man's raw energy.

They drove down the following evening, arranging it so that they arrived as night fell, when there was hardly any moon. Krink had scoped the place out over the course of the previous week, and just that morning he'd parked a Fiesta just round the corner with three cases of beer left in plain view. He knew it wouldn't be long before someone jimmied off the door – a Fiesta really is a sardine can with an engine – and Krink had arranged that forty cans were well and truly adulterated. It only took ten minutes for them to spot the booty and a total of eighteen to get it all stashed in the house. He presumed that they wouldn't be hanging around before necking the lot.

They parked on a verge about a mile from the estate, playing a game as they crossed the fields and hedges of making no sound whatsoever, not even the crackle of a twig breaking. With Krink it was a taught craft, a skill about which he was inordinately proud.

With Kamosiwe it was instinctive. Here was a man who could hit a macaw's heart across the reach of a broad river with a dart so hard that the bird would explode in a supernova of scarlet feathers. Each man listened out for the sounds of the other messing up, but smiled as they realised that they were walking within thirty yards of each other without hearing so much as a hint of footfall. Krink heard the brittle snap of a twig and felt ready to congratulate himself when he saw the heavy head of a cow silhouetted against the next field. He also realised that his friend was moving back and fore across the field in the most subtle oscillation, weaving his concealing way. They met at the stile, as agreed without so much as a whispered greeting. Krink felt that warmth again, a pleasure in the man's companionship and the assured way he disported himself even though they were going up one-to-eight against a pack of heinous racists. The Yanomamo people weren't exactly known for being tall, but there was a proud haughtiness in Kamo's step. They each took a separate alley way towards the house of their intended prey and Krink's ears strained to hear the man's tread among the broken glass but there was nothing, just velvety silence.

There were two of them outside the house, smoking cheroots while sitting down on the seat they'd stolen from the old people's home. The young Indian left them sitting there, stonily slumped as the curare paralysed their central nervous systems. Two down, fourteen to go. Krink meanwhile had got himself into a position where he could see what was going on inside the house, training his night scope on all of the front rooms: one a TV room where they were watching a porn film set in a South American zoo with an improbable sequence involving a tapir, then the kitchen where four men were standing up drinking beer and in the toilet there was a man seated down. Krink thought he'd rise to the challenge of taking him out before he had time to clean himself and so he slinked as a shadow behind the dustbins and with the gentlest of motions swung himself around a post and into position.

He'd spotted that the window was slightly open, enough for each hand to flick in a pebble each, guiding the loop of fishing twine into place so that Krink could yank it back so swiftly that the man wouldn't be able to so much as yelp before the neck was severed with the sheer brutal force that Krink's hands and ankles could muster after years of training. He felt tendons split like chicken bones and heard the thump of a body hitting the floor. Krink stilled his beating heart, waiting for the men in the kitchen to register the sound but their voices were raised against the sound of a Skrewdriver CD. He noted they were just opening the doctored beer, giving him a sense of impeccable timing. He ducked below the window ledge and crawled around to the front door where his friend was waiting for him. They'd agreed they would go in together. Krink brought out his rice flails and waited for the screams from the kitchen as the hallucinogenic beer worked its mental misery. It was a punctual drug – always kicking in after five minutes of drinking the poison. They would see all manner of things. The men in the front room went in to the kitchen to see what was going on and Krink and Kamo slipped in. Kamo picked up a heavy ashtray on a metal stand and crunched it down on a bonce even as Krink poleaxed another with a brick he'd picked up on the way in. The men in the middle room didn't know what hit them and the two attackers were moving with such speed and, well, grace that they didn't know what they'd hit them with either, but just at the point where they thought they'd go upstairs to mop up stragglers someone on the landing opened up with a Kalashnikov, but not before Krink had heard the tell-tale click of the safety catch being taken off and hurled Kamo into the kitchen before the staccato burst of bullets tore up furniture and smithereened the aquarium, where one of them bred terrapins.

The two of them found a bunch of loon-eyed crazies in the kitchen, limbs flailing as they dealt with their mental demons. One was in a nightmare where he was being chased by himself, or a doppelgänger around his childhood home, where he knew from bitter experience – when his angry father came looking for him with a poker yanked out of the fire – that there was absolutely nowhere left to hide. Another two were cowering, one trying to avoid the strafing of Messerschmitts as he shared a water-filled ditch with some tadpoles, while another, who couldn't swim, had just fallen off the back of a ferry. Krink decided to not put them out of their misery for a while, even though he could have dispatched them with the deftness of a poacher taking rabbits out of a net, and decided it was time to deal with the man with the submachine gun. He rounded the corner and hurled a flash grenade up the stairs and bounded up as the magnesium lit up the landing in the equivalent to a solar flare and saw the man shielding his eyes, although seconds too late now that his retinas had been crisped. Krink sliced him and went to check the other rooms, as his friend took on the strongman of the house, with Krink having wagered that he couldn't deal with him without a weapon in less than five minutes. It was already turning out to be a Titanic slugging match with the huge man raining down blows on a skull that seemed to be reinforced with titanium set on neck muscles which transformed into shock absorbers. The Indian hit the man's nose three times but the man swatted him away as if he was a fly. But the young Yanomamo sensed it was time to summon up his anaconda familiar.

The great snake reared ten then twenty feet above the man and opened its mighty mouth. Just the sight of the enormous gaping maw with fangs as big as bull elephant tusks was more than enough to get the man to drop his guard and as the body crushed his rib cage like a crisp bag, Kamosiwe could hear the distant voice of Krink suggesting they should high tail it out of there. The forensics team, when they arrived the next day, would be able to scratch grooves in their heads as they tried to puzzle out what the enormous sloughed-off snake skin was doing there, although the red-eared terrapins moving across the linoleum floor of the kitchen misdirected their thoughts for a while, before one of the newest members of the team pointed out that the snake had to be fifty metres long if it was a centimetre.

Krink and his partner ran across the field as the police sirens dopplered up the valley. They gunned the car over the hill and then drove at a sedate pace past sleeping hamlet and slumbering village to a trucker's chip shop where the radio was switched to a police channel and they listened to the barked excitement coming through the static as they wolfed down two substantial meals.

A half hour later Krink phoned the message 'The birds have returned to the nest' through to the answer phone of a man who knew another man who knew how to get the news through to the women who would by now have known all about the commotion, but Krink wanted them to know that this was a free service. Holding Kamo's hand, as they sat in a lay-by waiting for the drive-in movie of the sunrise to begin, he thought it was the least he could do. Even as the Amazonian moved in to reply with a tentative kiss.

Marigolds

It was called a mountain – Mynydd Mallaen – but there weren't enough tightly packed contour lines on the Ordnance Survey lines to make it so. It was hooching with Transylvanian bald-necked bantams which had escaped from Billy Kerry's coops down the valley and where they'd rapidly established a colony. They screeched like demons and threw up dust devils as they hunkered down on the ground. There they threw earth over their feathers to suffocate ticks. The birds attracted alert platoons of foxes and feral cats with claws like Freddie Kruger, nearly as sharp as metal. Despite the attention of these predators, the bantams were sufficiently alert and fecund to grow in both number and audacity. Some even attacked magpies and one suicidal bird, not long out of the egg, actually rode on a cat's back for a few yards before falling off.

Local legend had it that it was a place of druidical sacrifice. When the mists settled as a cloak – as they so often did on these brackened ridges – some swore blind you could hear screams coming out of the quarry. One old man, more fanciful than the rest, even said you could hear a thud as bodies hit the ground.

And then there was the taciturn ghost of Christmas Evans: the woolly-haired preacher who sometimes opened the door of the farmer's Land Rover, shuffled inside, helped himself to a lift as far as the milk churn at lane's end and then got out without so much as a Biblical bye your leave.

One Friday, in a convoy-cum-cavalcade that was as noisy as it was colourful, they arrived: the advance guard of the intentional community, the commune. The three vans, with their spiral decorations of rams' heads and swirling painted suns 'n' stars were a vanguard of intent, rolling in on twelve bald tyres. These vehicles weren't going anywhere else after this: this was journey's end. Through a gap in a blackthorn hedge, Tryfan watched them. The cantankerous farmer was already thinking about how best to frighten them away. He had seen off people before and some were running still. He wasn't scared to use his gun.

The travellers' vehicles were state-of-the-art clapped-out. Exhausts sounded like mortar rounds in south Lebanon. Some of the stragglers, such as an old school bus from wartime Maidstone, made emphysemic sounds as they went through the gears.

Tryfan was a man who smelled of old teabags and septic tanks; an utter stranger to soap and washing. He had been decidedly unhygienic ever since his mother – herself as unwashed as the Atacama desert – had warned him about the dangers of cleanliness. In a toad croak she would proclaim that it was only people with black hearts who washed, and that the Devil eats black hearts on toast, with a pint pot of ale to wash it down.

A shadow passed over Tryfan's heart as he remembered her advice after, what, forty years? Forty years since mam had been lowered into ground so wintery-hard five men had had to pickaxe open a grave for her over the course of two whole days. Even then it was so shallow they had to cover it in rocks to thwart badgers. Mam fach, what would she think of these charabancs and men with hair like women who were setting up camp within two hundred yards of the house? On the hill, the sacred hill! She wouldn't like it. She wouldn't like it one bit and he could hear her now, in a whisper that came out from under the rocks and slithered over to reach him: 'Get rid of them, Tryfan, and do it soon. These vermin have no right to be on land your great-grandfather bought with all he had. They don't belong here. This is where we work and this is where we're buried.'

That night the visitors played flutes, ate home-made bread and told each other stories. After the children were finally asleep the adults drank cider and laughed about their misfortunes on the road: how they had been refused service at one garage by a man with rampaging B.O. who called them bloody yuppies and how Maggs had tried to wind down the window of his van to make a hand signal and the whole door had fallen off as they headed west on the M4!

That night Tryfan couldn't sleep because of the sound of drums, a nocturnal samba played by a recovering crack head called Trevor, coupled with the peals of laughter coming from a Volkswagen camper full of people drinking magic mushroom soup, with extra mushrooms. In the van, decorated with all the fruit known to man and a couple of species more, their hilarity was matched by the strength and persistence of the visions they each had: swimming with talking seals in the bladderwrack surrounding holy Iona, daybreak rainbows and enchanted children playing a gamelan of tiny tinnabulations, cardboard cut-out mountains receding into the for-never-ness of somewhere too far away and a city where nonsense was the only logic so cars ran on cheese. Boy, those mushrooms from the edge of Cadair Idris were good – real brainmashers and neuro-scramblers. Magic, truly!

In fitful sleep Tryfan hatched his plan. In the morning, well before even the early rising cockerel had opened his eyes and before the dew had lifted from the burdock leaves, he was down in the sheep byre taking a carborundum to a scythe. When he lopped the head off one of the strangers' dogs they would feel no pain, but would run around silently.

Tanrallt farm was at the very base of the 'mountain' and by one of those accidents of geography was actually at sea level. If you took a step inside the farmhouse you'd see what any self-respecting nineteenth century novelist would call a hovel, with its soot-layered walls' lack of any decoration. There was a pair of jugs from Delft, most probably a gift from the squire to Tryfan's mother. Squire, indeed! Tryfan himself was born out of wedlock – *plentyn llwyn a pherth* – a child born in either copse or hedge. The owner of the big house's carnal appetites were well known, and his fearful whip was known for miles.

As Tryfan set out with murderous purpose, his

scythe crooked under his arm, he spotted a heron fighting with an eel it had caught in the pond. The bird gulped and tried to find purchase on the wriggling fish with its serrated bill and eventually managed to manoeuvre it down its throat, where it continued to struggle in the bird's crop even after the bird took flight.

When he followed the line of ash trees he heard a beautiful voice singing out and he saw the girl, Rachel, listening to a tape player inside the van. He was being seduced by a mellifluous song by Janis Ian.

'At seventeen', went the refrain.

Tryfan listened so intently he wanted to still his beating heart. It was a tune pure and fulfilling. When it was over he heard a man's voice and presuming it was the girl's father summoning her he raised the collar of his coat and headed back to the farm.

When he was ten he had met a girl in the fields. One April day he had given her some marsh marigolds wrapped in a cone of paper. She threw them away with scorn and a scathingly cruel laugh. They lay there for months, until the flowers became mere smears of green on the stones and the paper became mulch, a leftover wasp-nest. After that Tryfan left the ways of love to other men who found wives and had children while he ploughed his solitary furrow.

Once a week Myfyr, the deaf-mute tenant of Mysgryllt Fach, would call to see Tryfan and the two of them would exchange visual pleasantries, nodding like metronomes at each other as the fire settled into its own crackling rhythm in the hearth. He sometimes bought a load of peat from the gypsies, but with times hard and thumbscrews on, he was trying to extract heat out of sods of earth he'd cut out back. The place soon resembled a cheap fish smoke house and the two of them coughed like calves.

Tryfan mimed the girl singing and Myfyr made a phallus with his fist but Tryfan didn't laugh. The girl's song had touched his heart. He was far too old to be thinking of taking a wife and certainly not one that young. Anyway, women were forever decried by his dead mother as an enemy of his inheritance.

Outside the window, the old preacher Christmas Evans tapped on the glass, hoping for a crust and perhaps even a glass of ale, but despite the length of his yellow fingernails nobody could hear him inside.

In the morning Tryfan slinked down towards the vans where everyone was still fast asleep, other than the dogs with their wormy skin and decayed teeth. They had been up early to massacre bantams and the dogs were chewing away at innards, their mouths all blood, glue and feathers.

Tryfan was wearing the suit he wore on the day of his mother's funeral. As he walked up to one of the caravans he patted his mother's wedding ring in the left hand pocket. The song had made him feel alive, like the first drifts of snowdrops illuminating paths through dank stands of oak.

He knocked on the door of her caravan. The door opened and a man as shaggy as a caveman stood there, entirely naked, half asleep and aggrieved. Ken was the woman's partner. He stared at the old man as he offered the ring on an outstretched palm.

'Piss off you old pervert. I've seen you skulking

around the bushes, spying on us.'

Tryfan was hiding the ring in a ball of his fist. Hesitantly, he said he wanted their address.

'Address? You stupid old coot. We're on your land.' He then sensed something to his advantage so he added 'Her name is Rachel. Now fuck off.'

The old man nodded his head. It was enough for him that he knew her name; a sort of triumph. He walked away with satisfaction in his gait, his fingers laced into each other.

When he arrived back at the house he went up the dusty ladder into the loft and went to get the gifts. Three days later a small parcel arrived at the yellow caravan, handed over by a bemused postman who had recognised the writing as Tryfan's: his near-Gothic script scrawled ornately on all the correspondence he generated as secretary and main deacon of Gerazim chapel. The postman gave it to the girl without a word. There was a note to accompany its contents.

Dear Rachel,

Please find enclosed my mother's jewels. They were intended for a wife should I ever take one. Please accept them with my sincerest good wishes.

Yours,
Mr Tryfan Jones,
Tanyrallt Farm,
Five Roads,
Carmarthenshire

By now the caveman next to her was roused from his narcotic slumbers. The two of them looked at the pearls, the brooches and lengths of gold necklace. Neither said a word, quietly sizing up the other. What would they buy? He needed more drugs. She loved him despite the cloud of violence that always trailed after him. He'd get his own way.

It was Myfyr who found the old man at the base of the well, where the water had been the sweetest in the shire. He was dressed in his best suit, his hair was drenched and his body had begun to give off gases. Myfyr had looked everywhere, desperately shouting for attention despite his ruptured larynx. Mumph! Mumph! He'd cried as he ran up the lane and out towards the old milking parlour. Then he found the dogs, yapping around the stonework.

What is love? What is longing? Love is an old man with two broken tibias lying in a well where, in spring, old people would come to tie ribbons on the twigs surrounding it; visual echoes of a pagan past. And him a deacon and all. And in love, too, for five whole days in a life.

Estuarine

Jerry Lee lit a cigarette and surveyed the river as it cut across the marsh. A magnesium sky brightened up an expanse of reens and ditches, edging the layers of cloud with halos of lemon. He was happy and excited as his love was on her way.

As he dragged in the tobacco smoke, a green sandpiper rose from a pool full of silage, its bottle-green back vividly radiant against the whiteness of its tail. Wheeooo! Wheeooo! It was like the briefest snatch of a Vaughan Williams melody.

His smoke mixed with the vista. Hereabouts, the houses are classic Dutch gables, built by hydrologists and engineers with names such as Cuyp and Hooek, who came here in gangs two hundred years ago to canalise and drain all three estuaries. They connected the grips, the smallest gullies, with the field ditches which then ran into the reens and finally into the rivers. The houses and reclaimed land were protected from the seeping wateriness of the estuary by the Bank O' Lords, an earth embankment that runs dead straight, north to south, from the main road to the dank forestry plantations set on the dunes.

In the nearest of the three houses to the main road, in the lee of the bank, Jerry Lee is getting ready for a date. He had arranged for Bella to come to see him, a woman his mother described as 'that Jezebel from Burry Port' and that's when she's feeling kindly. At other times, she'd slurred her dismissively as the 'prostitute', or, archaically, as that 'fallen woman', which sounds more comical than lacerating, especially in his mother's budgie voice. Why Jezebel? Because Bella is an unmarried mother and his mother has a sense of moral outrage powered by Old Testament lightning.

Bella, or Bee comes to see him every Friday and she is all he can think about during all the days in between. Her teasing presence worries him like a cat playing with a captured sparrow. The marshmallow skin. The extraordinary, high cheekbones. The tide wrack aroma of her intimacy.

Jerry Lee's mother, of course, stays well away at weekends. She loves her son. At home she suppurates with rage and spite, spluttering like soup on a hot ring.

Bella is due at half seven. At six o'clock Jerry is still lying on the bed recovering from his labours. He had picked an acre of root vegetables by hand and chopped a formidable pile of wood. He'd been tempted to use the chainsaw to save time but as his mother often joked, the exercise makes you limber. He also repaired three lengths of wire around the horse paddock.

He wanted to take a hot bath, to allow the salts to seep into his weary muscles, but he didn't have the energy to get up. Jerry stared at the repeated motif on the wallpaper above his head. It was a very British trio: a Guardsman in red tunic with a bearskin on his head next to a smiling Pickwickian figure astride a penny farthing and a young chimney sweep with huge teeth. The sort of wallpaper his parents would have actually spent a good deal of time shopping for. They were effortlessly eccentric. His father, Gren, designed fireworks and had adapted one homemade rocket so successfully that it was still in use as a safety flare by the coastguard service. He was the one who had insisted that his son be named after Jerry Lee Lewis, the hellfire rock 'n' roller who would sometimes set his piano on fire. His dad loved the guy, his flamboyance and heavy-handed playing style. Not that Gren listened to very much modern music. But he'd loved Jerry's flair.

His mother was famous, at least within the tight, concentric ring of her poetry readers, for having adapted the keys of her typewriter, so that when she typed, the words would have little tails and curlicues. A manuscript of her poetry looked like pressed ferns. Her publishers had to copy her volumes by lithograph rather than have them typeset. The words were beautiful to look at and to understand.

Jerry read a few pages of one of the books next to the bed, one of his burgeoning collection of what he called Old Tyme Religion, foxed books of theology and memoirs by fusty, self-aggrandised preachers. You could actually buy them by weight from a company that cleared houses for £4.99 a pound and he loved both the scent and the substance of them. And he liked the word they used in the catalogues. Avoirdupois. They were a master class in mildew and moths, thumbed by generations of lonely theology students aiming to find God by study, and a wife in some vestry.

With an hour to go before Bee was due Jerry summoned up some vestigial willpower and got up. This was a tiredness unfamiliar to him, and especially unexpected seeing as Bella was coming.

He stood on the porch outside and sluiced his chest and underarms using water from the green jug which was set to catch rainwater. He put on his best Paisley shirt and went downstairs where he put on a record of 'Saturday Night Fever', which he liked to sing along to. His bullfrog baritone hardly complemented the falsettos of the Gibb brothers but the music set the mood. He spun on the balls of his feet and shook his hips with sufficient vigor to spring them from their sockets. He got his breath back with a beer and then lit a cigarette.

Looking out at the silvery threads of water that wove through the grasses and mud of the salt marshes he conjured up Bee's exotic face. When they first met she reminded him of a Hopi Indian he'd seen in a favourite *National Geographic* article about the reservation at Three Mesas, Arizona.

That first time she was buying masonry nails in Jones' Hardware and he'd pointed her in the direction of a more dependable brand than the 'One Hit Wonders' she had in her hand, apologising in the same breath to old Mr Jones, who raised an eyebrow as he did him out of a sale. For the first time in his life Jerry summoned up the temerity to ask a woman if she'd like to join him for a drink and she said 'yes' disarmingly quickly. Mr Jones looked ruefully at his display of nails, now as useful as a chocolate teapot.

On that first date Bella teasingly told him she came from Mongolia and said her mother was a hundred and nine and lived in a tiny apartment in Ulaanbaatar. He'd looked it up in the library on the way home and in one of the photographs he found there were ghastly apartment blocks that sprouted in that awful Soviet style as if the builders had decamped from Ceausescu's Romania. But the people in the photographs had the same physiognomy as Bella, high cheekbones and eyes seemingly protected from wind whipping in over the steppes. She might not have been teasing, after all. She was certainly an exotic in these parts, where in-breeding was evident in many a cross-eyed leer. Like Hawkins the milk, who had the same birthmark on his cheek as his two uncles.

Bee and Jerry Lee were still at the Velcro stage of their sexual relationship, still ripping and tearing clothes off each other's backs as soon as they set eyes on each other, working up a frantic sweat of need and lust and more need.

When she arrived, wearing a raincoat and little else, she attacked him with the usual energy, but he was spent after his exertions out among the crops.

'Bee, you've got to stop... I'm having three bloody thromboses here, all at the same time. Stop that or my heart will burst,' he bleated, his lungs rasping like soldiers in mustard gas, but she took his pleading as part of some elaborate theatrical foreplay. Bella dismissed his imminent extinction and continued with the job in hand.

When it was over and Jerry's breathing had slowed down she looked at him with an intensity he hadn't seen before, a mix of benign enquiry and fateful fascination.

'It's not just physical you know, Jerry. There are several more dimensions to this.'

'Survival's the dimension I'm most intrigued by. I fear I'll be disappointing you all too soon. The age is there.'

She laughed, throatily as she loved that expression. The age is there.

'Nonsense, you're only in your fifties and I've read somewhere that with the right vitamins you'll be able to stand proud well into your eighties and beyond.'

'Beyond?' gasped Jerry.

A part of him was relieved. A part of him was shocked by her openness, her complete lack of shame.

Their first real date had been a whist drive in Cwmsych where Jerry had won the star prize, a turkey so big he reckoned they'd cross bred it with a cassowary. Bee offered to help him carry it to his car. As they struggled through the doors of the church hall he noticed her green eyes again and surveyed her extraordinary physiognomy, and the faintly Japanese way she'd applied mascara.

He couldn't remember how she'd invited herself back, a ruse about teaching him to baste the bird, but when they got to the house she proffered a half bottle of Italian red from her handbag, saying she's squirreled it away for special occasions.

She was all adventure. That night she offered to dress up as a nurse, but Jerry had too many associations connected to his mother's time in hospital: cardboard urine trays, the snap of surgical gloves going on. But she stayed nevertheless, and it was the first time in his life that he greeted the dawn with a wide-awake woman at his side, and one rolling a post-coital spliff at that. He needed his post-coital asthma inhaler. On the marshes, roosting wigeon sent out the occasional whistling cry, nervous of foxes and falcons.

During the next few weeks he felt he was on a sexual wurlitzer and he really was in fear for his heart. After all, his grandfather had suffered from a dodgy ticker. And he worried about his mother turning up unannounced, to find Bella performing a come-on in shrink-wrap latex, or that outfit with the leather straps.

The days tested his patience, with time slowed down so that the afternoons unwound before him like pizza dough. He hated the waiting game, but Bee insisted that they should keep some sort of distance, even though she admitted that she really delighted in her time with him and stressed the appeal wasn't just the pneumatic sex. She'd sent him a garland of gardenias to thank him for the garlic chicken he'd made for her the previous Saturday. They had arranged a new adventure for the next weekend. From bed to the sea-bed, as he cryptically put it.

'There is nothing – I repeat nothing – that can compare with being out in the bay at night.'

Jerry was lowering the sea kayak into the water,

as tiny foamy waves lapped at his boots. 'You can, well, commune with nature. Is that life jacket comfortable or do you need me to loosen the strap?'

Bee thought of other dates she'd had with men and none compared with this moment – the fullness of the moon lighting up glistening sandbanks and this muscular man with the unusual name holding the kayak steady as she ventured in. She hadn't told him she couldn't swim as he made her feel as if she could do anything. As she sat down he sealed her in the sleek craft with a rubber coverlet and then got in himself. He took out the oars and soon he had struck up a purposeful rhythm and was taking them out towards the hump of land beyond which lay Rhossili and the Worm's Head.

On the surface of the water there was an unexpected phosphorescence but he explained that it was actually quite common. It was just that very few people ever ventured out to sea at night, other than some stalwart mackerel fishermen. He chatted away, pointing out items of interest, although most of the features on land were really only outlines in different shades of black. From time to time she lost what he was saying because of the wind and when that really seemed to be picking up she asked him whether it was time they turned back. He assented, realising much too late that the sea was choppier now and he cursed himself for being so besotted by this woman that he forgot the rules of basic safety.

Bee kept mum and tried to enjoy the moment and live in it. Jerry had found a strong rhythm now and was taking them away from choppy waves to a patch of millpond stillness, where he said you could hear pirates from a long sunk galleon. And indeed, as they scythed through water like icing glass there was an inexplicable sound, unearthly and fit to take one's breath away. And then he saw what it was and whispered to her, he whispered to her with all the amazement of a child finding its voice for the very first time.

'It's a whale!'

She saw the drifting hulk and then heard an ethereal song, which must be able to carry to the end of the sky, so perfect was its register. And then she saw the smaller shape in the water, breaching almost silkily and moving close in to its mother. And in a tiny gasp, it started to answer her song, with a little plaintive cry of its own. It was a moment of all magic, a complete and enveloping epiphany and the two human beings in their frail kayak were spellbound by the sound.

And then, just as suddenly as it had appeared, the whale lifted its tail and dived down. Jerry Lee sat stock still and the sound of his excited breathing melded with Bee's breaths, audible even within the soughing of the wind.

They might have stayed there a century or just five minutes, but the magic was slowly dissipating. This majestic, enormous beast, this nature, this thing of ineffable mystery diminished to tadpole size and swam away into memory.

A whale and its calf, unexpected in Carmarthen Bay, under an arc-lamp moon. And then, above, two shooting stars raced in tandem across the void and Jerry wondered if they'd been sent by his father, flashing messages from the King of Fireworks who had passed away exactly a year ago. It wouldn't surprise him. He had a flair for timing his pyrotechnics just right. He imagined his old man lighting the touch paper just before his eyes closed in on themselves, like ferns curling away from summer.

They had to negotiate choppy water on their return. The little craft lurched from side to side now, and soon Bee was being heavingly sick and Jerry was finding the rowing hard work as he strained his sinews to beat a path back to land. It started raining, too, and there was the occasional hailstone. His eyes were stinging even as he oared on, the work heavy now, pausing only to bark out reassurances to Bee who was having the worst time of her life. Hard on the heels of the best time in her life. She was scared now, scared and cold and very aware of the fact that she only had a yellow badge for swimming the width of the municipal swimming pool when she was still in school.

'How far are we?' she asked, trying to contain her voice down which was tempted to shriek.

'We'll be there in no time,' said Jerry, his lungs working like bellows now, the strain catching up with him. He couldn't see anything at all, but trusted his instinct which had been unfailing in the past.

They made landfall an hour later and by then Bee was past fear and Jerry's muscles were close to spasm. He had barely enough energy to help Bee out of the kayak and haul the slim craft up the beach, aware that the tide was now on the turn, and, ironically, the weather was just beginning to improve.

As she began to find her legs on land, Bella turned to Jerry Lee and confided in him that she could not swim. He took her in his arms and pulled her in tight towards his torso.

'I am a woman transformed,' she said, as she settled within his embrace.

In the dunes a light flickered from a bonfire and Jerry imagined a circle of people, burning a Steinway that had been carried in by the tide, the ivories crackling in the heat, the strings zinging as they burst.

He pulled Bee closer to him, trying to get rid of the sound of the lacquered wood splintering. In her eyes he could see tiny orange flecks, reflecting the flames in the dunes. But there were also fathomless depths, ones to explore for ever.

Another piano string burst, louder than the others, sufficient to startle the crows in their roost in the conifers behind the beach. From far out at sea came the plangent sound of whale call. Jerry gave in to what was happening to him, as she kissed him, her hair black foam in the moonlight, her beautiful eyes marooned beyond all description. He gave in because she was the one, and her lips seared his, hot and wonderful, slick with brine.